Tris grabbed two fistfuls of wind. She twisted them around each other, following the lessons taught by Lark and Sandry: spinning made weak fibers into strong thread. Finished, she backed up to the inner edge of her lightning-circle and stood her windthread at its center. Grimly, she twirled her finger clockwise. The wind began to whirl.

Bit by bit it drew in pieces of other winds, growing taller and wider. When it was of a size to crowd Tris out of the circle, she sent it into the air and let it touch down in the blanket of thorns on the other side of the wall. Twigs and sticks fought their way up the growing funnel as it ate vines, becoming a thorny kind of armor.

"Aymery," she growled to make herself angrier, and slammed her creation forward. It sprayed against the glasslike wall, grinding at it. Again and again she threw her creation at the barrier. . . .

The Circle of Magic Books

TAMORA PIERCE
Circle of Magic

Tris's Book

SCHOLASTIC INC.

New York Toronto London Auckland
Sydney Mexico City New Delhi Hong Kong

Acknowledgments

Thanks are due to my father, Wayne Pierce, for his help and advice in my research on black powder; to my mother, Mary Lou Pierce, for her gardening advice (used more in the last book, but still appreciated); to Rick Robinson, not only for sea matters but for fast-turnaround proofreading and reader reaction; and to Tyndulf the Peacemaker for the harbor chain. As always in this series, thanks go to Thomas Gansevoort, particularly in matters of weaving and smithcraft. Thanks also to Victorian Video and the Cumberland General Store as suppliers of invaluable source materials in such arcane areas as smithcraft, companion plants, and weaving and spinning.

No part of this publication may be reproduced, stored in a retrieval system, or transmitted in any form or by any means, electronic, mechanical, photocopying, recording, or otherwise, without written permission of the publisher. For information regarding permission, write to Scholastic Inc., Attention: Permissions Department, 557 Broadway, New York, NY 10012.

ISBN 978-0-590-55409-1

30 29 28 27 26 25 24 23   13 14 15 16/0

Printed in the U.S.A.   23

First Scholastic trade paperback printing, September 1999

The display type is set in Yolanda and Sophia.
The text type is set in Berling Roman.

Map by Ian Schoenherr
Interior design by Cathy Bobak

Circle of Magic

Tris's Book

1

She was pressed—*jammed*, really—into a corner formed by chunks of stone. Someone's knee poked into her thigh on one side. Someone else's foot dug into her calf on the other. There were four of them, and a dog, trapped in a bubble in the ground. The first part of an earthquake was just fading, and the rest about to roll over them like high tide pounding the harbor walls.

Sweat poured down her cheeks and back. Half turning, she thrust her hands palm-flat on either side of a crack between the stones. Calling to the power inside her, she sent her magic through the gap.

Earthwaves were coming her way, small ones in front, bigger ones behind. Their force heated dirt and stones, spreading everywhere. Her bones felt like huge rocks, pressed together so hard that something would have to give. They would slip alongside one another with a crash, forcing buildings and streets and whole cities into new shapes.

And the heat, the earth's heat was cooking her and the friends whose bodies pressed against hers. The hot waves roared through the ground, gaining strength as they traveled. When they hit, she could choose between being roasted or crushed: the earth around her small hollow would clench like a fist—

Trisana Chandler lunged out of bed, throwing off the thin sheet that had been her only covering, jumping for her open window. Dangling half out of it, she gasped in the open night air. She was aboveground, in her attic room in Discipline cottage, at Winding Circle Temple in Emelan. The earthquake was ten days gone, and she and her friends had lived to talk about it.

But the heat! No wonder she dreamed of it still, with the air dead around her. Every door and window in the attic was open, but not a breath of air stirred under the thatch. It was scarcely cooler outside.

Voices reached her ears on the tiny puffs of air that did touch her. Once she'd thought the voices meant that she was going crazy. Now she knew they were only pieces of real conversations that took place somewhere, carried to her by the wind. It still made her a little nervous to hear them, although they spoke mostly of everyday things.

"*Aymery Glassfire, I am impressed.*" The prissy and dry-voiced speaker was a man unknown to Tris. The name "Aymery" pricked her—she had a cousin Aymery, but his name was Chandler, not Glassfire, and he was hundreds of miles away, at the university in Lightsbridge. Aymery was a common name. "*The learned men who wrote these letters give you praise indeed. I could no more refuse to allow you the use of our library than I could fly.*"

Tris shook her head, trying to get that voice out of her ears. To be hot *and* bored was just plain too much!

The simple act of moving captured a fresh puff of air, drawing it close. "*Novice Jaen, how could you allow our stores of bandages to fall so low?*"

"*But—Dedicate Willowwater—I didn't know I was to check the other storage rooms—and so many bandages were needed after the earthquake—*"

"*Oh, don't cry, girl. We'll have to contrive something, quickly.*"

"*The foretellers don't expect more trouble, do they?*"

"*When we're out of bandages, who needs to read the future to know more trouble will come?*"

Tris growled. Magic was supposed to be grand and powerful, not a question of the contents of linen closets! Sticking her fingers in her ears, she rubbed fiercely. When she stopped, the voices were gone and she was hotter than ever.

Somewhere in the hazy, dark blur in front of her weak eyes was the twenty-foot-high wall that enclosed Winding Circle. From its top, she might catch a real breeze.

Tris stripped off her nightgown and yanked her lightest cotton dress over her head. Once it was on, without regard for her dress or the floor, she grabbed her water pitcher and dumped its contents on her head. For a few blessed moments she was cooler.

Groping under her bed, she found her leather slippers and jammed her feet into them. Unwilling to wrestle with her sopping red curls, she tied a scarf around her head, so at least her hair would be off her neck. Last of all, she groped on her dresser top for her brass-rimmed spectacles. Jamming these onto her long nose, she headed for the door and yelped with surprise. One of her housemates stood there, leaning on the frame. In the shadows, the black girl was almost invisible until Tris was right on top of her.

"It's the strangest thing," the newcomer commented softly. "You're bat-blind without those spectacles, but you know where everything is, so you don't even need a candle to get dressed."

"You *could* have made a noise, Daja," grumbled Tris.

Her housemate ignored her. "Someday the boy's

going to decide to joke with you and move everything while you sleep. Then where will you be?"

"Better ask where *he'll* be if I catch him," retorted Tris. "And don't you go suggesting it to him, either. Why are you still up?"

Daja Kisubo raised her hands and stretched her solid body as high as she could. If she stood tiptoe, her fingers almost touched the top of the door frame. Younger than Tris by almost a year, she was still a hand's length taller than the redhead's four feet and seven inches. "He doesn't need *my* help coming up with pranks," she replied, her lilting voice dry. "He's got too many ideas of his own. Why get dressed?"

"It'll be cooler on top of the wall. Maybe Lark will let me go there for a while."

"How do you know it will be cooler?" Daja inquired.

"Am I the weather-witch around here or not?" Tris demanded irritably, hands on hips. "I *know*."

"Wait, then." Daja turned and entered her own room, just across the attic.

Tris grumbled, but followed the other girl to lean against *her* open door. Daja's room already had light of a sort from a candle set on the family altar in the corner. Daja changed to breeches and a shirt and shook out her various short braids. Slipping her feet into sandals, she blew out the altar light, then followed Tris downstairs.

5

It wasn't all that late. One of the women in charge of Discipline was still awake, writing a letter. She wore only an undyed cotton shift as she worked— her Earth-Temple-green summer habit was tossed carelessly over the table. Like Daja, she was dark-eyed and dark-skinned, though her skin was a lighter shade of brown. She wore her glossy curls cropped short; they fanned out to frame an almost catlike face with broad cheekbones and a pointed chin. As late as it was, as hot as she was, she still gave the two girls a smile, which they returned. Even Tris, with her moods and her temper, liked Dedicate Lark.

"Just for an hour," Lark told them, digging in a habit pocket. She produced a round iron token that showed the bearer was outdoors with permission and handed it to Tris. "If it's still this hot when you come back, we'll set up pallets for you on this floor."

Someone who sat in the shadows near the front door got up, startling Daja. It was a boy, dressed only in light breeches. His skin was even more golden brown than Lark's, his almond-shaped eyes a startling gray-green. He wore his black hair coarse-cropped no more than an inch or so from his scalp. His nose was short and straight, his mouth firm and slightly down-turned at the corners. "Lark—" he began.

"Yes, Briar, you may," Lark replied, tired but amused. "Put some shoes on."

Grumbling, the boy entered his room.

A head with sun-streaked brown hair dressed in

6

two braids poked out of the room across from Briar's. Sleepy eyes of a bright, cornflower blue peered at them. "I heard voices," the girl said, and yawned. A young dog, all ivory curls, elbows, and tail scrambled into the main room from hers, dancing frantically and whining.

"Sandry, we're going up on the wall to cool off," Daja said. "You want to come?"

The light brown head nodded; its owner vanished inside her room and closed the door. A minute later she came out, wearing a blouse, skirt, and slippers, pinning up her braids under a scarf.

By the time she was done with her hair, the boy reappeared, hopping as he tried to yank a sandal over one foot. The other was already shod. "You girls better not take forever to get ready—" he began, then realized that they were waiting for him. He switched his attention to the dog. "You better not keep me waiting, Little Bear."

Sandry, laughing, shoved the boy out the front door ahead of her. The pup yelped and followed them, as Daja and Tris brought up the rear.

The last one out the door, Tris stopped and looked back. "Lark?"

"Yes, dear?"

"W-would you like to come? With us, I mean?" A part of Tris was dismayed: What had she turned into? Two months ago, she *never* could have made such an offer to anyone, particularly not an adult.

7

Two months ago she had come to Discipline cottage. Now she had days when she wasn't sure who she was, but she knew that she liked the change.

Lark smiled. "Thank you, but I'm to do the fires at midnight services. Some other time, perhaps?"

Blushing hotly at her lapse into affection, Tris nodded, and ran to catch up with her housemates.

Panting as they reached the top of the wall, each found an open stone notch to sit in. Instantly they realized that Tris had been right; it *was* cooler up here, and they had a fine view of the cove below Winding Circle's south gate. Their dog flopped onto the walkway behind them with a happy sigh.

"How much more of summer is there?" Daja asked, once she'd caught her breath.

"It's just the second week of Mead," replied Sandry. Yanking off her scarf, she undid the ties at the ends of her braids and combed her hair out with her fingers. "Two more weeks after this in Mead, then all of Wort Moon."

"Maybe even most of Barley, too," Briar chipped in. "Rosethorn says all the omens are for a long summer, and a short autumn." His teacher, Rosethorn, was the other woman who watched over Discipline.

"What are you doing up here?" A pair of guards trotted down the walkway from one of the towers that punctuated the wall. Dressed in the red habits of those dedicated to serve the gods of fire, they carried long staffs capped with broad, two-foot-long blades as weapons.

The friends got to their feet and moved closer together. The dog sat in front of them, thwacking the stone with his tail. Digging in her pocket, Tris found the iron token and passed it to Sandry. Things went better when their noble did the talking for the four.

"We have permission," Sandry explained, showing the token to the guards. One side of it was marked with a D, for Discipline cottage; the other showed an engraved bird and a thorny branch for Lark and Rosethorn.

"But this should be only for one child," argued the woman. "There's—"

The man was far taller than his partner. The four watched, amused, as he bent down to whisper in her ear. Though he kept his voice soft, they still heard him mutter, "It's *those* children. The four mages. They often run together."

Briar puffed out his chest. He liked being called a mage, as if he were a man.

Sandry planted her hands on her hips. "I am Lady Sandrilene fa Toren. You have my word that we *all* have permission to be here," she informed the guards.

"Only Sandry," Daja muttered in Tris's ear. The other girl covered a grin with her hand and nodded in agreement.

The female guard blinked at Sandry. "That kind of thing will work much better when you've got some height on you and a bit more nose." She returned the iron token.

Sandry covered her nose, which was little more than a button.

"Don't lean out over the wall," advised the man. "Don't get to playing in the notches, either." The guards each petted the dog and walked on.

"You know, if you want, I'll pull your nose every day till you get a beak like your uncle's." Briar slipped his fingers under Sandry's and tweaked the end of her nose. "It'd be my pleasure, really."

"Thanks ever so, Briar," the girl told him sourly.

"I wouldn't offer if I didn't mean it," he assured her, gray-green eyes wide and solemn. "Honest."

Tris climbed up into her notch again. Pushing her spectacles up, she eyed the array of sea and islands that stretched before them. Even with the moon just beginning to wax toward full, she could see details at a fair distance: the watchtower on Bit Island, for one, and the glassy smoothness of the Pebbled Sea. A flash of light over shadowy humps was the Maja Island lighthouse. To the east, a mile or two down the long arm of the Emel Peninsula, gleamed the beacon on Pirate's Point.

"Look at this, will you? A good, steady wind and not a cloud in the sky." Tris loved storms. She took clear skies as a personal insult.

Sandry leaned on her notch. "Pirate weather," she remarked softly.

Daja made a face. "Dirty *jishen*."

"What does that mean?" Tris asked. "*J-jishen*. It's Tradertalk, isn't it?" She always wanted translations for new words in Daja's native language.

Daja shrugged. "I don't know—tick? Louse? Leech?"

"It's something that feeds on others and then kills them," added Sandry.

Tris looked out to sea. The wind shifted a hair, carrying the scent of trees to her sensitive nose as it passed directly over the islands.

It also carried voices.

"*This thing's heavy.*"

"*Quiet!*"

Tris bit her lip. Not again!

"Did you hear something?" whispered Briar.

"*Why'd they just pick me and you?!*" panted the complainer. "*This thing needs at least two more—*"

"*The less that knows, the better, y' lazy cod's-head! Now stow it!*"

"It's two men," Daja muttered, looking around. She wasn't a nervous girl, but she knew the sound of shady dealings when she heard it. "No one's in sight—"

"Tris is hearing something on the wind," Sandry told them.

"And we hear it, too?" Briar scowled. "We never heard it before."

"Before the earthquake," pointed out Daja. "Before we combined our magics—"

11

"Hush!" snapped Tris. Closing her eyes, she fixed her mind on the speakers. Whatever they carried, it was heavy: both Whiner and Gruff Man were gasping. They were scared, too, for all that Gruff Man would deny it. She heard the fear in their whispers.

"Now what?" demanded Whiner. He sounded better—they must have put down their burden. *"Do we knock?"*

"I swear by Shurri Fire-Sword—"

The noise of clattering bolts and creaking hinges—the sounds of a heavy door being opened—interrupted Gruff Man.

The other three children came to stand behind Tris. With her concentrating, the talk was even louder in their ears. As she heard the conversation, so did they.

"You're late!" hissed a female voice. *"Ye wan' us t' get* caught?"

Daja wrinkled her nose scornfully. The woman was drunk.

"Git that thing in here, b'fore some un comes! Watch changes in an hour, an' sometimes they're early!"

Gruff Man and Whiner grunted, as if they'd picked up their heavy burden. A breath later, the door closed.

Tris faced the others. "You heard?"

"Like they was standing right here," Briar replied. "And none of us could do that hearing trick before."

"We're one now," Sandry murmured.

"Not all the way one," protested Tris. "When you

fell this morning, I didn't know. When Briar stole that muffin from the coldbox, my belly didn't fill up."

"The muff would've gone bad anyway," grumbled the boy.

"We haven't really done a lot of magic since the quake," Daja pointed out, tugging on Sandry's braid. "If we had, maybe we would have found out—"

"Found out what?" snapped Tris.

"That perhaps we know what goes on with each other's *magic*. We can't do the same things maybe, but we know what happens in all our magics." Daja sighed. "Something complicated. Simple things don't happen to us anymore."

"Maybe it will go away," Tris said.

"What of the bleaters we're hearing?" asked Briar. "Can we tell what they're up to, or where they are?"

Tris shook her head. "I just hear voices—I can't tell where they're from."

"Smugglers, maybe?" Daja suggested. "Most islands with guard posts have some kind of smuggling going on. Guards always think nobody pays them enough." She had spent years among those who lived and worked on the sea and knew the practices of all kinds of people.

"It *could* be smugglers," replied Tris.

"Forget about it," advised Briar. "No use sticking your neb where it don't belong."

"Can we leave noses out of the conversation?" asked Sandry wistfully, tugging the end of hers.

Rusty hinges creaked on the wind. Tris held a finger to her lips, and the four stopped talking.

"—here's the cord." The Drunk Woman sounded as if her liquor was wearing off. "*But if ye lay it on the ground, will it burn? We—*"

There was a thunk, a sound like a cleaver biting into uncooked beef. Then came a choking gasp. Briar made a face. He'd heard people stabbed when he was a street thief. "The woman's dead," he muttered.

Tris gasped.

"*If we leave her in the open they'll find her!*" That was Whiner. "*They'll know something's—*"

"*Stow it,*" snarled Gruff Man softly. "*Once we're clear, the mage'll light the cord and—*"

Something roared and thumped at the same time; light blazed across the sky. The four children flinched and stared out over the water. The Pirate's Point lighthouse was a pillar of fire. Closer to home, just a mile away, the watchtower that capped Bit Island was a blazing ruin.

The dog, startled out of his nap, began to bark furiously.

Finished with his porridge, Briar yawned. He was exhausted. The four had been kept on the wall for another hour after the towers had exploded, answering the questions of first the dedicate guards, then their superiors, then the four's main teacher, Niklaren Goldeye, and Moonstream, the Honored Dedicate who ran Winding Circle. It meant they had gotten very little sleep by the time the temple's great clock summoned everyone to the new day's work.

Beside him, pale gray eyes half-open, Tris patted her remaining porridge with her spoon. She had managed to pin up her mass of wiry red curls, but they were already struggling free of their restraints. She had gotten even less sleep than Briar. Tired as she was, the image of those spouting flames had stayed in her mind, keeping her awake for a long time. From the way the adults had talked the night before, they had no idea of what caused the explosions.

Across from Tris, Daja Kisubo toyed with a plump braid. She didn't care about how rested she was, or about the explosions. She wanted to start the day's chores. With those finished, she could go to her teacher, the smith-mage Frostpine, for another lesson in working metal. Today he was to beat gold into thin sheets, and she looked forward to that. She had very good feelings toward gold—not for its value, as her Trader-kin liked it, but for its friendliness and its willingness to forgive mistakes as she handled it.

Next to her, Sandry neatly folded her napkin and placed it beside her bowl. As always, she sat with her back perfectly straight, her lively eyes examining her friends. Daja had to be thinking about smithcraft, Sandry decided. The only time Daja ever looked dreamy-eyed, as some girls did when they thought of a special boy, was when she considered tools and metal and fire. Briar, of course, wanted more sleep. Two months wasn't enough to turn a night-hunting thief into a daytime gardener. And Tris, frowning into half a bowl of cereal, what was she thinking of? Tris was always asking questions about things. She had asked a great many of them last night and gotten no answers. Perhaps that was why she scowled at her porridge.

"I once saw explosions like that," Sandry remarked, fingering the small pouch hanging on a chain around her neck. "A shed with some barrels of flour caught fire, and they blew up. The shopkeeper told my parents that if you bottle up flour and then fire it, that's what happens."

Tris glared at her with ice-gray eyes. "*Flour* blew up two stone watchtowers?"

"If you had enough of it?" Briar covered a yawn.

Sitting next to Sandry, their puppy whined.

"You'd think we never fed you, Little Bear." At the head of the table, Lark ran a hand through her own glossy curls.

"He's a growing boy, aren't you?" Sandry gave the pup's ears a scratch.

"That's what scares me," Lark and Daja said together. They smiled at each other.

Sandry grinned ruefully. Little Bear had been small enough to fit in her lap when they had gotten him. Now he could sprawl over her lap and Daja's and still prop his chin on someone else's leg.

"Where's Rosethorn?" Briar demanded.

"Water Temple," was Lark's reply. "They still have her brewing cough syrups." She got to her feet, shaking out her green habit. "She says you know what to do today—"

"Weeding," was his gloomy reply. "Because in summer it's *always* weeding, weeding, weeding."

Lark smiled. "Well, at least there isn't as much as there was yesterday, then."

Briar snorted, half laughing.

"Dedicate Willowwater has asked me to meet her at the loomhouses," Lark continued. "Why a Water dedicate wants to see me at an Earth Temple building—"

Tris pushed her bowl away. "She's out of bandages, or almost out," she mumbled. "Some novice wasn't keeping track of the stores." When she realized she heard nothing but silence, she looked around. Lark and her friends watched her with fascination. "I *heard* it, all right?"

"How come *we* didn't hear it, then?" Briar demanded.

"I was by myself," retorted Tris. "It was before we went out. Maybe you have to be close to me for it to work."

Lark tucked one of the girl's tumbling red curls behind a hairpin. "Sometimes I think we haven't even begun to see your gifts, Tris. We—"

Little Bear erupted in a series of ear-piercing yaps. Scrambling, he raced out the front door.

"It's someone he knows," Briar announced. "See? His tail wags him."

"No, Little Bear, do *not* jump on me," a familiar,

brisk voice commanded. "No! I *said*, *no!* That's a good—now don't start again."

A lean white man with long silver-and-black hair that hung loose around his shoulders entered the house, pointing down at Little Bear. The pup half walked, half wriggled behind him, whimpering happily. He knew there was no way that Niklaren Goldeye would let him jump up and wash his face, but Little Bear still hoped for a chance to show affection.

"Good morning, everyone," the man said.

Tris ran to him and tugged on one of his spotless white linen sleeves. "Niko, did you find out how the towers were destroyed?"

"Tris, do *not* wrinkle my shirt," Niko ordered. "Let go." His tone was stern, but his black eyes, set deep underneath thick dark brows, were kind. "As it happens, I am here on just that errand. Lark, I'm sorry, but I need her to come with me right away."

"She has chores," Briar pointed out. "Same as all of us."

"Washing dishes," added Daja.

Niko shook his head. "It really must be now, and I require Tris. We have to look into the destruction of the watchtowers. We may even be gone for midday."

Tris held very still, fingers crossed, praying to go.

"I'll wash *and* dry," Sandry offered, "if she'll do the same for me another time."

Lark put her slim brown hands on her hips. "Is that good enough for you two?" she asked Daja and Briar.

Daja shrugged. "Sounds fine."

The boy scuffed a foot on the ground and scowled. "I don't know," he replied sullenly. "It don't seem right."

Tris glared at him.

He looked up and grinned broadly. "I gotta stop teasing you," he remarked. "It's too easy. There's no sport in it."

Tris stuck her tongue out at him, then ran upstairs for her shoes.

"I'd finish the chores soon," Niko told Daja. "Frostpine has a special task of his own. I saw him at the main dining hall—once he's settled a few things, he'll be up here."

Daja got up quickly and began to stack the bowls.

An hour and too many stairs later, Tris and Niko stood before what had been the Bit Island watchtower. The walls, which had once soared forty feet in the air, were now two and three feet tall and pierced with gaps. Only the edges of the ground-level flooring were left; the boards were gone, leaving the cellar open to the elements. All of the inner stones were soot-streaked, their surfaces chipped and cracked. Tris noted splashes of crimson where Niko had said the Duke's men had found bodies earlier. An odd smell lingered in the air: a sharp, smoky odor, charred wood, a hint of burned flesh. Touching a blackened chunk of rock, she got soot on her fingers. Sniffing them, she blinked. The smell was in the soot.

Niko crouched at the cellar's edge, staring into it as he smoothed his bushy mustache. In spite of their hot climb, he looked cool and elegant. He made a sharp contrast to his red-faced, sweating pupil, clad in an ill-fitting green muslin dress.

Tris fumbled to re-pin her curls up and out of her way. "It looks like the tower shattered, doesn't it? But how? A mage?" she asked.

Niko looked up at her. For a moment, she wasn't certain he'd heard the question. Then his dark eyes softened. He caught a hairpin that leaped from her hand. "I should have made you wear a hat."

"It would be in the ocean by now. What did this?"

He sighed. "*No one* should be able to work de-structive magic here. The magic protections were in the foundation. This—whatever it was—destroyed even those spells. See how the stones spray outward from here? The force pushed them *away* from itself."

Tris crouched beside him, interested. "Where were the protection spells?"

"You can't see them?" he asked. "They're all around—what's left of them."

She wiped her face on her sleeve. "*You* see magic, not me."

He stared at her, shocked. "But it's easy. I haven't taught you how?"

Hot and itchy as she was, she had to smile. "Well, *last* week we were picking up after that earthquake. Two weeks *before* the quake you were running everywhere, trying to find the source of all the disaster omens the seers were getting. Before *that*, we studied tides and stars." She flapped her skirts to give herself a little cool air. "No—I don't believe we ever worked on seeing magic."

"Really, I had meant to be *organized* in your studies," he muttered. "Unfortunately, events have swept us along . . . and for now, I *still* don't have time for that particular lesson." He thought for a moment, then stuck out a hand. "Give me your spectacles."

Tris shrank back. "I *need* them."

"It's just for a moment."

Slowly she took them off and passed them over. Now she couldn't even see what he drew on the inner surface of the lenses with his finger.

At last a breeze swept by, ruffling her hair. Three curls promptly jumped out of the pins holding them, and voices came to her ears:

"My boy, I had begun to think that something had gone amiss." The voice was a man's, cold, almost metallic.

"Forgive me, my lord. This is the first moment I've been sure of my privacy. I'm in place." Another male voice, and one that was somehow familiar. Not *very* familiar, like Frostpine's or Niko's, but it was a voice she'd heard before. Youthful, sure of itself . . .

"We are not yet ready to move. Await instructions," the cold voice ordered. *"Do your part, and your debt will be paid."*

The breeze was gone, and the voices with it. The sound was replaced by something that cheeped faintly, a *real* noise, not one plucked from the air by some weird power inside her. She looked around. Was there a bird up here?

Niko yanked out his handkerchief and gave her lenses a going-over. "Don't you ever *clean* these?"

"Of course I do!" She snatched the spectacles when he offered them, and shoved them onto her nose. "Now what?"

"Don't look directly at that heap of stones," he ordered. "Look at them out of the corner of your vision."

Obediently, she turned her head, putting the rocks at the edge of her left eye—nothing. She twisted her head at different angles, without results. Niko made a choked noise that could have been a laugh, or a sneeze. She glared at him.

Silver flickered at the edges of her lenses. With a gasp, she turned to stare. The silver vanished. Slowly she looked up, staring at a cloud as it wandered overhead.

There, at the edges of things, was a glimmer of moon-pale light.

Soon she had the trick of it: to look at everything in general, and nothing in particular. With her eyes just slightly unfocused, she could see flickering bits of light everywhere on the rocks around them, symbols and pieces of letters. "How long will this last?" she wanted to know. "The magic on my specs?"

"As long as you have those lenses," he replied. "Just remind me to teach you how it's done before you get new ones."

Something cheeped again. Tris peered for its source. Was she hearing things?

"Remember I said I needed your help?" he asked, getting to his feet. "To find out what happened, I need to see into the past. It's one of the great spells—if I do it alone, I'll be so drained I won't be able to move afterward, let alone go to Pirate's Point. If you would lend me some of your magic, it will be easier."

She blinked at him. "What must I do?" She had lent some of her power to Sandry once, but she had no idea how it had happened.

"I'll call it forth, as long as you agree to let me do it. Not just in words, Trisana. You must agree from within. You have to trust me."

She looked up into his eyes, set in their heavy fringe of black lashes. Trust him? He was her teacher. He had seen inside her and told her she wasn't crazy—after her family had said for years that she was. Because of him, she lived where she was wanted; she could ride the winds. "Sure, Niko."

He took her hand. Immediately she felt something,

a tug, or a twist. Through her spectacles, she saw a thread of light run through her fingers and into his, where it joined a river of fire inside him. The air tightened. Still holding onto her, Niko picked his way around the tower, one hand held palm-out in front of him. Pearly threads spun away from his fingertips, passing through air and stone around and ahead of him. Once he and Tris had come full-circle around the hole in the ground, they stopped. The threads continued to flow over the land until they covered the entire hilltop like dew-wet spiderwebs.

When he released her, she could still see the thread that connected them. It followed Niko as he stepped to the edge of the cellar, drew his belt-knife, and made a cut on both palms. "Any time you need to give a spell extra strength, seal it with blood," he explained casually, as if it hadn't been his own flesh he'd gouged. "Since we are mages of principle, we use our own. Some have been known to use the blood of others, willing or not." He watched as crimson droplets fell into the gaping cellar. "Should I ever hear of you indulging in such practices, Trisana, you will regret the day you met me."

Tris had one hand over her mouth. She didn't like blood, and there was something about Niko's coolly cutting into himself that made her stomach roll. "You don't have to worry about me, Niko," she told him once her belly settled. "Honest."

He smiled grimly. "I trust not." Taking a deep breath—Tris felt her own lungs expand—he closed his eyes.

A flickering image appeared in front, around, and in some spots even through him. In it, the tower was whole. Two men in hats and cloaks walked into the picture. They carried something large and heavy, wrapped in canvas. A door opened in the tower's base, and a woman in a guard's uniform beckoned them inside.

"It's Whiner and Gruff Man and the Drinker!" cried Tris. "It *has* to be!" The night before, she and the others had told Niko about the conversation they'd heard on the wall.

The vision wavered, breaking up: Niko was shaking. Tris glared at the glowing line that still ran from her to him, until it thickened and shone more brightly. He took a deep breath and stood straighter; the tower reappeared. The men walked out of it, the uniformed woman behind them. The men's burden was gone, but one of them carried the free end of a cord that led back inside. He put it down and helped his companion kill the guard. They didn't see a burst of fire that set the cord ablaze. The flame ate its way along the cord and into the tower as they dropped their victim on the ground and argued. Then came the blast. For a moment Tris thought she could see the tower come apart, stone by stone, each piece etched in fire.

The image vanished. Tris closed in as Niko staggered and put an arm around his waist. Helping her teacher over to a large rock, she got him to sit.

"What was that?" she asked him, when he was settled.

He fumbled for his water canteen and drank from it thirstily. He needed both hands to steady it.

"I don't know," he replied at last, passing the canteen to her. "I've never seen—or heard—of anything like it, not in all of my fifty-three years."

They rested for a while, talking. At last Niko got to his feet. "I don't think I could work that spell again, but I should look at Pirate's Point anyway," he said. "Let's go."

She was following him to the stairs when she heard the same cheeping sound that had caught her ear before. Now it was close by and growing faint rapidly.

"Wait," she called. Carefully she searched the tumbles of rock on her left. In a niche made by stones gleaming with traces of magic, she found a birds' nest. One chick was still alive—she'd been hearing its peeping cries. It shared the nest with a dead brother or sister.

"A starling, I think," Niko said, looking over her shoulder. "They sometimes have a second brood in midsummer. The parents are probably dead, if they nested here. This one will die soon."

Tris looked at the nestling. That's not right, she

thought, digging for her pocket handkerchief. He didn't ask to have his home destroyed. Kneeling, she flattened the linen square on a rock and reached for the nest.

"Tris, think a moment," ordered Niko crisply. "You can't save it."

"Why not?" With a gentleness that she rarely showed to people, she eased both hands under the wad of twined grass stems.

"Because it's nearly dead now. See how young it is? It barely has pinfeathers. If it lives, it will need warmth and *hourly* care. It isn't ready to survive on its own."

"Then I'll help. I'll feed him—I'll do whatever I must." Resting her hands on the cloth, she drew them away gently, until nest and occupant rested on the handkerchief. "It's not *his* fault his parents got killed."

Niko sighed, and offered his own pocket handkerchief. "You can return to Winding Circle. As I said, even *with* your help, I can't work a second timespell at Pirate's Point. If the site looks like this, though"—his wave took in the sooty wreckage all around them—"I think we can guess what happened. Hold the nestling up." He opened his water canteen and carefully poured a tiny amount of liquid into his palm. Gently and precisely, using his fingers as a slide, he rolled a few drops of water at a time into the bird's open beak as Tris raised the nest for him. When the chick closed its mouth and sank back, Niko told

Tris, "Now cover it. Keep it warm and out of drafts—I know that much. For the rest—"

"I could ask the dedicates at the Air Temple. They keep birds." Slowly, a bit at a time, she got to her feet and tucked the covered nest into the corner of her elbow.

Looking down at his student, Niko grinned. "Actually, try Rosethorn. She often finds nestlings in her garden. She's even raised a few."

Tris stared at him. She was *terrified* of Rosethorn. The auburn-haired woman had a sharp tongue and a quick temper.

"Do you want to be running to the Air dormitory every hour? Rosethorn will know what to do. I *still* doubt it will live—"

"He."

"Tris, no one will be able to tell until it's ready to mate what sex it is."

"Then it might as well be a he as an it," she told him stubbornly. "Its are dead things. Shes and hes are alive."

"Oh, very well. I haven't time to argue. If you insist on trying to save it—him—"

"I do." Tris gulped, thinking of what lay ahead. "I hope Rosethorn will help me."

"She will. She likes birds *much* more than she likes people. Let's go, then. You need to feed and settle him, and I need to go to Pirate's Point."

Steadying her new charge with her free hand, Tris followed Niko down the stairs.

If Tris had looked across the thousand feet of water that separated the island from the land, she would have seen three people on the rocky slope below Winding Circle's walls. One of them was Daja, dressed as she had been at breakfast, in her lightest brown cotton breeches and shirt, with a crimson mourning band around her left arm. With her, in the red habit of a Fire dedicate, was her teacher, the smith-mage Frostpine, and his white-clad novice, Kirel.

Frostpine was black like Daja, his skin a few shades darker than hers. What hair he still possessed grew in a lion's mane around a shiny bald crown; his beard sprouted wildly from his chin. The sleeves of his habit were rolled up and secured with ties, revealing a pair of arms that rippled with wiry muscle and big, strong hands. Kirel was half a head taller, white-skinned and blue-eyed, with long, fair hair. Big-bellied and heavy-armed, he was the kind of young man who looked as if he belonged in armor with a two-handed sword slung across his back. Before they had left the cottage, Daja had made sure Kirel was slathered with ointment to keep him from burning in the sun; a bottle of the stuff was in one of the baskets on the mule that the men had brought with them.

"Take off your shoes, and get on your hands and knees," Frostpine told her. "The more of you that's in contact with the ground, the better."

She thought he was crazy, but she obeyed, placing her sandals to the side. Out here, the sun beat down like a hammer. She was already sweating enough that the drops tickled as they rolled down her cheeks and back.

For a moment she thought she saw a fishing boat at the corner of her eye, off Crescent Island. When she took a quick glance, there was nothing to be seen.

"Remember what we did once, hiding lumps of different metal under cloth?" he asked.

Daja nodded. "You made me guess what was under the cloths, and I knew what metals they were because of my magic."

31

The mage's hair bounced as he nodded. "Do the same thing now. Search under you for any trace of metal. Not raw metal, but metal that's been handled, and worked."

Sweat dripped into the dirt from her face. "It's too hot."

"Too *hot*?" he cried, white teeth flashing in a broad grin. "Child, we are *black!* Black people are *made* for heat, to *thrive* in it—just as pallid boys like Kirel are made for snow and frost."

Kirel halted. He had been walking a hundred yards away, holding a long metal divining rod out in front of him. "I hate snow," he retorted calmly. "And if you weren't crazy, Frostpine, you'd hate *this* weather as much as I do." Reaching up, he tied back his hair with the braids that hung on either side of his face.

Daja covered her grin with her hand. She loved working with these two. They were as relaxed and cheerful as the men of her own family had been, joking about work as they got it done.

Frostpine shook his head. "Shurri and Hakoi," he muttered, calling on the goddess and god of fire, "defend me from people who don't know how to have fun. Let's give it a try, Daja."

With a nod, she put her hands palm-down on the raw earth. For some reason trying to smell metal helped her to find it, so she sniffed deeply. Was that a trace of . . . ?

She inhaled again and yelped as the scents of

32

copper, iron, silver, and gold flooded her nose. Eyes watering, she sneezed and kept sneezing. A hand gently pushed her aside; a handkerchief was tucked into her fingers. Three more bursts pushed themselves out of her lungs, making her wonder if it was possible to suffocate while sneezing.

The earth quivered under her, then shifted. Her throat closed with terror: earthquake! Her sneezes halted abruptly as she thrust herself backward. The last shake had been just ten days ago. Were they about to get another?

Small dirt clods rolled downslope. Wiping her eyes, she saw Frostpine standing where she had knelt. His arms were stretched out, his hands parallel to the ground. He shook them, gently, as if he sifted ore through a screen. Below him, the patch of ground shook, gently, in the same motion.

Daja sighed with relief. It wasn't a fresh quake or tremor, but magic, pulling something out of the ground. The dirt began to take on a strange, meshlike pattern. Kneeling, Frostpine dug his fingers into the earth.

"Will you get that corner?" he asked, pointing to the edge of the patterned dirt. "It's a wire net."

Going to the spot he'd indicated, she dug her fingers down about an inch, until they passed through a metal web. "Got it," she told him.

"When I count to three. One—two—*three.*"

They dragged the net from the ground: a large

piece three feet long and four feet wide. Daja blinked. The net was a shimmer of the metals she'd smelled, twined into fine wires and knotted like cord. At half of the spots where the wire threads met, a tiny mirror was set. The whole piece fell over her fingers as if made of water.

"What on earth is it *for?*" she demanded.

Kirel walked over to them, holding three or four smaller pieces of net. "I've never seen anything like this."

"Has either of you wondered why, in the last four hundred years, no pirates have ever attacked Winding Circle?" asked Frostpine.

"I am—I *was* a Trader." Daja swallowed hard. She'd almost said "I am a Trader," but that part of her life was over. "We didn't think about how *kaq* could or couldn't defend themselves." Sandry would frown at her for using the word *kaq*. Like many words the Traders used to describe non-Traders, it was not flattering.

"I lived in north Lairan," added Kirel. "We didn't know anyone could fight in ships." He grinned and winked at Daja.

"Time was this net covered the entire bluff, from the harbor wall"—Frostpine pointed right, where the protective wall stretched from Bit to the cliff—"to where the Emel River empties into the sea. There's more in the earth in front of the walls, too, a mile-wide belt that wraps around all of Winding Circle.

Whenever the Dedicate Council thought there might be pirates or land-raiders in the area, they woke the spell-net like this." The man hummed a weird tune.

Daja and Kirel gasped. The net that Daja and Frostpine held vanished. Only the open sea lay between them—or were they high in the air, over the sea? Daja still felt metal cutting into her fingers, but made no connection between that and the distant view of—

She could *not* be seeing Dupan Island. Nidra was eight days from here, off the coast of Hatar. Still, she ought to know it. She'd sailed from the island's harbor just five months ago. . . .

It wasn't just the view. She could smell land, sea, and normal ship-smells like tar and wet rope. The deck rocked under her feet, and one of her cousins was scrambling up the mast, whistling.

She blinked, and she held a metal net in her hands. Kirel rocked back dizzily. "I was climbing Blacktooth Mountain," he whispered.

Daja dropped the net and wiped her eyes on her sleeve. She'd been on Third Ship Kisubo, whose crew was also her family. They were gone, shipwrecked and drowned in a late winter storm not long after leaving Nidra.

"I'm sorry," Frostpine said, putting a hand on her shoulder. "I can't control what people see or feel when the spell-net is woken. It's powerful, though, as you've learned. Pirates have spent *days* in the same place, until they were too weak to avoid capture when the spell was released. And this is the first time *I've* been on the wrong side of the net when the spell is worked."

Daja shrugged. "It was just the sneezing that made my eyes water," she lied. "But listen, my friends and I were up and down this bluff all the time, before the quake. We never saw *anything* like this."

"You weren't supposed to," replied the mage. "It works only when triggered. And it's worked so long, and so well, that most of the Council had forgotten until I reminded them that it might have been damaged when the bluff dropped into the sea. We're to find as much of it as we can, and bring it in for repairs." He sighed. "If most of it's in pieces like that"—he nodded to Kirel's small pile—"then we'll need more help."

"Have there been omens of pirates?" asked Kirel, worried.

"Who needs omens?" asked Frostpine. "We had an earthquake. Everyone's defenses are in a mess. What pirate would want to lose an opportunity like this?"

As briskly as any housewife, Frostpine took the large piece of net and brought the ends together, folding it up like a blanket. Daja helped, thinking over what he'd said. Once the net was folded into a neat bundle, the man loaded it into the empty basket on the mule. Kirel added a stack of smaller pieces and went back to combing his part of the ground. Daja went to a clear spot several yards away from where she'd discovered her first piece of the net and knelt.

Something tugged at the corner of her eye. Was that a fishing boat? It had a three-cornered sail, at least. She turned her head to look straight at it.

The sea was empty. There was no boat in sight.

Sandry was just finished with the dishes when Lark returned from the loomhouses. "Was Tris right?" asked the girl.

Lark nodded. "I just can't understand how Water Temple supervision is so lax that a novice could empty four storerooms, but—Oh, that's the Waterfolk for you. All froth and bubble, and they get diverted by the tiniest stone in their paths." She shook her head. "Worse, Dedicate Vetiver tells me that her two best weavers suffered broken bones *and* broken looms in the quake, and the others are still turning out cloth and blankets for the countryside. She'll put one more weaver to bandages, but they still need us."

"I'll do all I can, of course," Sandry replied, "but you know I can't weave. You haven't had the chance to teach me yet."

"That's all right," Lark told her with a sigh. "What we have to do won't exactly involve weaving. And bless Mila and the Green Man both that you're so strong, as young as you are. We could never do this otherwise. Come on. Leave Little Bear with Briar."

She led Sandry across the spiral road between

Discipline and the two great loomhouses. Entering one through an open door, they came to a small workshop, apart from those rooms where Sandry could hear the clack of a dozen weavers at work. In this chamber a strange assortment of things had been set up. A few rolls of bandages had been placed on two long tables; more rolls filled a large basket on the floor. Other baskets held giant spools of linen thread. A comfortable chair was placed beside each long table. The shutters were thrown open to catch what breeze the day might send their way. A pair of novices sat on a bench next to the door, to run errands.

Lark sent them to the kitchens at Winding Circle's hub for tea. Once they were gone, she took Sandry's hands in hers.

"What I'm going to ask is strange, but you can handle it." She took a deep breath. "I *will* teach you how to weave properly, when I can. What we do today is *not* real weaving. It may look like it, but it's a cheat. If you rely on magic without learning to do ordinary weaving properly, there will come a day when your great magics won't hold—magic can't teach you how to weave right. The novice always has gaps, loose threads, or places that are too tightly packed in her cloth, and all those things weaken the spells you include in the work. Do you understand?"

"Of course I do," replied Sandry. "I don't want to take shortcuts. I want to learn to weave well."

Lark smiled and cupped one of Sandry's cheeks

with her hand. "That's why you'd be so good at weaving—you care for the work, not just the magic." She looked around. "Magic, though, is what we need today—and magic worked fast, which isn't what I want you to learn about *magic*, either, now that I think of it." She began to open up a roll of bandage linen, pulling until the narrow cloth was stretched across a third of the length of one table. "You see those spools of linen thread? Bring some here. Put them in a row across the cloth you already have. Take the loose ends and draw them until they hang over the far end of your work surface."

Sandry obeyed. Watching Lark, who did the same thing at the other table, she arranged spools end to end across the narrow part of the bandage, so the thread followed the length of the cloth and went on past it, all the way to the end of the table and over.

"If you're trying to strengthen a wall against destruction, or bring a company of people together, this is a way to do it," explained Lark, coming over to check what she had done. "We weave magic, and get the stone, or the hearts of the people, to follow it. Here we guide the thread to continue the original pattern of the cloth, like a vine growing along a trellis. We grow new cloth from the stump of the old." She deftly put spools of thread on either side of first the bandage, then the long, bare threads. "These will be your weft. They'll run through the warp threads to produce a whole cloth."

Sandry frowned, turning these ideas over in her mind. "Could Briar and Rosethorn manage it? They grow plants on trellises. Flax and cotton both come from plants—I bet they could do this, too, if you end up needing more help."

Lark started to reply and stopped. Then she grinned. "If things get desperate, that's exactly what I'll do."

"Can't the other weavers try this?"

Lark shook her head. "Not all of them are mages. Even for the ones who are, this takes a different way of thinking about magic from what they're used to. *Your* ideas about magic aren't set as yet. For you it expresses itself through weaving cloth as easily as through putting a spell on the cloth once it's made. This kind of thing also takes a very strong mage."

The novices returned with their tea and a tray of cakes, fruit, and cheese: Dedicate Gorse, in charge of Winding Circle's kitchens, was sure that anyone who left his domain empty-handed would starve to death in short order. Lark sipped her tea, nodded, then told the novices to sit on their bench and be quiet.

Looking at what seemed like a half-ordered tangle of threads running north and east, Sandry winced. "I don't know if I can do it."

"Don't worry. I'll place the magical patterns within you. Clear your mind, and let the power follow the pattern steadily. Don't clutch at it, and don't let it run unchecked, or you'll have lumpy cloth. Watch the pattern as you work with it, so you can do it on your own later."

Sandry looked at her teacher and friend, her blue eyes deeply troubled. "Are you *sure* I can do it?"

Lark smiled. "It would surprise you, the things I know you can do. Now, clear your mind."

Sandry took a deep breath, fixing her mind on her lungs and nothing else, holding her breath as she counted to seven. Lark put the girl's hands flat where the spooled threads overlapped already-woven cloth and covered Sandry's fingers with her own. When Sandry exhaled to a count of seven, Lark joined her, to breathe and hold and release as she did. The sounds of beating looms and weavers' chatter faded; the scents of lint, oregano, and Ibrian broom flowers vanished; even their awareness of the intense heat faded. Sandry dropped into that calm with pleasure, knowing that she approached the source of her magic.

Lark was with her, holding what felt like a glowing net. If Sandry looked at it closely, it shifted under her gaze: first it seemed made of needles, then of cool liquid, then of simple thread. Lark pressed it into her hands and her mind, where it sank deep into the girl. Gently Lark nudged her attention toward the materials under their hands. Unwoven threads began to wriggle and crawl, like tiny snakes. The long threads that stretched over the seemingly endless wooden table vanished into already-woven cloth. Peering more closely, Sandry could see new threads crawl along old ones like roses on a trellis. When they reached open, unwoven air, the other spools of thread waited to snag them. Together all of the threads began to dance, weaving in and out.

Now she saw where the feeling of needles and healing liquid came from. Visions of wounds—cuts, gashes, round holes—rose from the pattern to fill her mind and run through her fingers. The cloth she wove must weave flesh, too, closing painful openings with threads of new muscle and skin. Where something had destroyed, her bandage would build new, healthy growth.

You're all set. Lark's voice rang in her mind. *Make sure they keep to the pattern in the bandage we started with. One hundred threads to the square inch. A simple tabby weave: in-out, in-out, for just the width of the cloth, and back again. It's all right if you're slow at first. Just keep control of it like you would if you were riding a frisky horse.*

I will, Sandry promised.

Lark drew away as Sandry continued to work. Her threads burrowed and twined together. Here, an inch from the original cloth, a double handful rushed into the same area like unruly children, working themselves into a gleeful knot. Sandry concentratred on them, nudging them apart, sending them in their proper direction, at the proper spacing for the weave. They fought at first, tightening their knot, but she refused to accept their rebellion. One at a time, she shooed them into their correct paths, until they were caught up in the overall rush of the weaving.

A distant part of her felt Lark start her own bandage. Later the novices replaced near-empty spools of thread with full ones, and rolled up the finished cloth. Sandry neglected even to thank them. Her attention was locked on the magic that flashed in and around her hands as the bandage grew, and grew, and grew.

Tris's luck, and she wasn't sure that she wanted to call it that, was in. For the first time in days, Rosethorn was at Discipline, not somewhere else, when Tris brought her nestling home. She had to steel herself to enter Rosethorn's workroom. She wanted to put it off, but her charge picked that moment to renew his frantic begging for food. Little Bear, lying gloomily beside the open door—Lark and Rosethorn had put charms in their shops to keep inquisitive puppies out—raised his head and thumped his tail.

The quiet conversation in the workroom came to a

halt. Then Rosethorn said, slowly and awfully, "I hear a baby *bird.*"

Carefully Tris stepped around the dog and through the open door. "Niko said maybe you could help me?"

Briar was with his teacher. Both of them stared at her. "Four-eyes, what happened on Bit?" asked the boy.

"Let me see," Rosethorn demanded, holding out a hand. Tris obediently passed over the nest. "I am *not* looking after birds," the dedicate continued. "Those twitterpated fidgets at Water tell me that unless I brew more decoctions and oil rubs there will be nothing short of disaster." Muttering, she shifted the handkerchief to look at the nestling as Briar and Tris rolled their eyes at each other. Rosethorn always talked scornfully of the Water Temple dedicates, just as Lark did at times. Weeks ago the four had decided that Water and Earth in human beings simply didn't mix that well.

"So talk," urged Briar as Rosethorn examined the nestling.

Since Niko had given no orders to keep what she had seen to herself, Tris explained about looking at the past and described what they had seen. "I think maybe five people were killed up there, counting the smugglers and that drunk guard," she finished. "You could tell where the dead had been."

Rosethorn went to a section of shelves. Reaching

high overhead, she got down a slender bottle. Like most things in the room, it gleamed silver-white at the edges of Tris's vision, casting more light than even the remains of the spells on Bit Island. Tris rubbed her eyes. It was bad enough that the south gate and the tower of Winding Circle's Hub had nearly blinded her. She hadn't expected to see so much magic, or such *powerful* magic, in the simple cottage where she lived.

"So Niko had you call up a vision of the past? That's a major working," Rosethorn commented, un-stoppering her bottle. "I need one of the thinnest hollow reeds we keep in that drawer." She pointed, and Briar obeyed the order.

"Niko did the spell-casting," replied Tris. "I just gave him my strength. He said I needn't come to Pirate's Point—we couldn't do it twice in one day."

She watched intently as Rosethorn accepted a short, hollow reed from Briar. Thrusting it into the open bottle, Rosethorn covered the opening in the dry end with a fingertip. She brought it over to the nestling and let a couple of drops fall from it into the bird's mouth. The youngster closed his beak, wheezing—then sat up straighter and opened his beak again. Rosethorn gave him another two drops.

"I have to be careful with this," she told her audience, putting the reed aside. "It's like drugs that give extra vigor, or dull pain—he'd come to need it, and not eat anything else. You have to give nestlings food that's close to what they get from their parents, or foods that are normal substitutes."

Rosethorn eyed Tris, delicate brows still knit in a frown. The girl forced herself to meet that very sharp gaze without looking away. "You understand, you might work yourself sick, and he'll still die," Rosethorn said at last.

Tris nodded. "Niko told me the same thing. I want to try anyway."

"He won't thank you, either, if he lives. Starlings—that's what this is—starlings are *annoying* birds. Their fledglings shriek when they're hungry. If they're old enough to walk and fly, they peck their parents until they're fed."

"There's gratitude for you," Briar commented with a grin.

"What must I do?" Tris wanted to know. "Tell me, and I'll do it."

"Hm. For now, feed him every fifteen minutes, until I tell you to change. Briar, you're going to see Dedicate Gorse—"

He clapped his hands. Next to Lark and Rosethorn, Winding Circle's chief cook was his favorite dedicate, a reliable source of both meals and treats.

"*Come right back,*" Rosethorn added sternly. "Slate and chalk, please."

Briar found both and gave them to her.

"Warm goat's milk—*goat*, mind; cow's milk is too

hard for them to digest—with a dab of honey for sweetening, at first—you can get those from our cold-box," Rosethorn told Tris. "Heat the milk in a small pan. Get it warm enough that a drop on your wrist feels *warm*, not hot. If it burns you, it'll burn him."

Tris ran to do it.

"Get one of the cup-shaped baskets and clean straw," Rosethorn ordered Briar. "Put them on the counter." She finished writing to Gorse as the boy found the things she needed. Giving him the slate, she said, "Don't run in this heat, but don't dawdle."

Briar nodded and left.

Tris was quick to put goat's milk and honey on to warm on the hearth. Unlike the other three children, who made a big job and a mess out of basic tasks, Tris had been doing household chores since she was tall enough to see over tables. Each family member with whom she had lived had made it clear that she was to earn her keep. She would never admit it, but these days, with lessons in magic and meditation to fill her time, she rather liked the quiet routines of dusting, washing, and even the mild amount of cooking done in the cottage.

When the goat's milk was just warm, she carried it into Rosethorn's workshop.

"Put it there," she was ordered. "There" was a wo-ven straw pad. Rosethorn was tucking clean straw into a basket with a rounded bottom. It sat in a wooden frame that kept it from rolling onto its side. "I made these a few years ago, when I saw that even if *I* found no birds, someone else would bring orphan nestlings to me. They need support on their chests and legs—a basket with a flat bottom and straight sides is no good."

Tris only stared at the woman. Since coming to Discipline she had feared Rosethorn's sharp temper and sharper tongue. Lark and Rosethorn were good friends, and Briar loved his teacher, but Tris couldn't begin to guess why. Was this the face of Rosethorn that Lark and Briar saw, when no one else was looking?

"H-how do you know so much about birds?" she stammered. "Do—do you have magic with them?"

Rosethorn eased her fingers under the nestling, who shrieked at the invasion, then lowered him into the fresh nest. "Don't *ever* squeeze them. Their bones, even their beaks, are very soft yet."

"I'll remember."

"Not everyone who loves a thing has magic with it, you know," Rosethorn said, dipping a finger in the milk. "Very good—exactly the right heat. Get that clean reed. Do what I did with the potion. Give him just a drop or two at a time."

Hands shaking, Tris put one end of the reed into the milk, closed the free end with a fingertip, and raised it. Taking her finger off the opening, she watched as all of the milk poured out. Trying again, she lifted her finger quickly, then closed the opening

49

again. Now she controlled how much liquid came out and could deliver it as drops, instead of a flood. Filling the reed a third time, she peered into the nest.

The youngster was cheeping. Was he louder? She prayed to Asaia, goddess of air and birds, and let two drops fall into the open beak. Startled, the nestling closed its mouth and swayed. He lifted his head and cheeped for more.

As Tris fed the youngster, Rosethorn said, "Gardeners—farmers—learn about birds, if only so they can tell which ones eat the crops and which don't. I started with nestlings when I was your age, on my papa's farm. All right, that's enough. He'll sleep for a while, but you'd better get ready to heat another batch of milk."

"Every fifteen minutes?" Tris wondered how she could do anything else if she had to see to her charge.

"Until he's stronger. If he improves, we can go to every half hour this afternoon. If he *keeps* improving, in a day or so, you can wait a whole hour."

Tris gulped. "How will I sleep?"

"Goose! Do sparrows and crows race everywhere at night? Chicks sleep with the sun. Come here." She went to the door that opened on the garden, and beckoned to Tris. "See that bird sitting on the roof of the well?"

Tris saw him, a handsome brown-black fellow who ruffled his chin feathers as he whistled loudly. He looked to be about the length of her hand, with yellow legs and a sharp-looking beak. When he turned, his feathers gleamed in the sun and showed off a multitude of tiny specks.

"Starlings. They're called that because they look like a field of stars. Insect-eaters—clowns. They imitate other birds—a lot of the local ones cry like seagulls. They form the big flocks you see swirling around at day's end. I have a soft spot for starlings."

The starling on the well said, "*Gaak*," and flew away.

"Come on," said Rosethorn. "We have to fix things so you can keep this youngster warm at night."

When he left Dedicate Gorse's kitchen realm in the Hub, Briar carried a loaded basket as well as a meat turnover to help him survive the long minutes until midday. If Rosethorn hadn't been willing to teach him the mysteries of plants, he would have been perfectly content to labor for Gorse—hot as the kitchens were in the summer—for the rest of his life.

When he was thinking of other things—the Bit Island tower, Tris's bird—he forgot that it was no longer important to hide when he had food. It had only been two months since he was a half-starved street boy. Looking for a dark corner in which to eat his turnover safely, he found a niche in the round chamber at the center of the Hub. The room was a plain, shadowy circle wrapped around a beautifully carved wooden screen that reached through the ceiling. Inside that wooden tube, a stair ran up as high as the great clock at the Hub's peak and down to the secret room called Heartfire, far underground. The wooden screen also enclosed a dumbwaiter, shelves on rope cables that carried messages from the seers in the far-seeing and far-hearing rooms in the upper levels down to this floor. When he'd come through on his way to the kitchens, two runners had been sitting on the floor, ready to carry any messages from the upper floors. They were gone now. Briar tucked himself into his niche and happily bit into his snack.

Something rustled in the wooden stairwell. Rats, he thought, putting a hand on a little dagger tucked inside his shirt. Back in Hajra, his old home, rats would try to take a meal if a kid didn't look like he could hang onto it.

Wood clacked. Gears moved, and Briar heard the rumble of the dumbwaiter. Just messages coming down, he thought, scornful of his jumpiness. As if Gorse would let rats near his kitchen!

There was another sound, under the rattle. Briar knew the scuff of a bare foot on wooden floors. He drew even further into the shadows.

The door in the screen opened a hair at a time. Briar caught a noseful of cinnamon scent and bit down a sneeze. Though he doubted any thief would have the sauce to operate here in Winding Circle, he knew professional thieves used cinnamon oil to baffle tracker-mages. It was expensive stuff. Beneath the cinnamon's peppery tickle he found another scent, one that was honeyed and slow: poppy.

Three weeks ago, Rosethorn had started to teach him magical uses for the oils in her workshop. "If you want to waste poppy oil, don't use it for medicine," she'd said then. "Use it for invisibility. It does more good as medicine, though."

Silvery light flickered. Someone drifted out of the stairwell, closing its door without a sound. Briar squinted. The light glimmered all over a blur that passed between the stair and the outer door. It traced a man's shape.

Rich man, he thought as the blur left the tower. Rich enough to afford cinnamon and poppy oils. Unless it's a student, raiding his master's oil stores. Two months wasn't long enough to erase his old ways, but it had taught him student-mages were always trying something they shouldn't. Winding Circle had more than its share of students, too, of every sort.

Putting down his basket, he went to the stairwell and opened it, eyeing the steps and the dumbwaiter ropes. The cinnamon odor was stronger here; he found spots of oil on the inner doorknob and on the wheels that raised and lowered the wooden boxes for messages. Shaking his head, he closed the door and fetched his basket from the corner where he'd left it. Students playing with their magic, he decided. Who else would try invisibility spells in the Hub in the middle of the day?

And how else could he have seen the person within the spell, unless it was a student who didn't quite have it right? Back in Deadman's District, he'd *never* seen the Thief-Lord pass invisible among his subjects, listening to their secrets and their plots against him. The Thief-Lord had always worked with the best spells money could buy.

The Hub clock struck the midday hour. He'd best get back home, so Tris could give her bird a little solid food.

The hide-and-seek ship was making Daja crazy. There it was at the corner of her eye whenever she looked up from her work, but if she looked straight at it, she saw only the Pebbled Sea, glassy and hazy with the day's heat. Ever since Tris had passed by on her way home, the ship seemed to hang out there, teasing Daja to look quick and catch it. By the time the Hub clock chimed the end of the midday rest period, she felt as if she'd looked up as often as she felt through the ground for more pieces of spell-net.

"Is something wrong?" asked Kirel. Frostpine had left them, questing for more of the net further down the cove. "You twitch like sand fleas are eating you."

"I've got an *azigazi* at the corner of my eye," she told him crossly, wiping her forehead. "It's as bad as sand fleas!"

"A—what did you say?"

"I'm sorry." He couldn't help being a *kaq*—a non-Trader, ignorant by birth—though she often forgot he was, because she liked him so much. "*Azigazi*. It's a vision, a false sighting. Out at sea they come when it's hot. White Traders say they get them in snow and sand fields. You see things that aren't real."

"A mirage, or a vision. *Azigazi*." He turned the word over in his mouth, as if he tasted it. "Could it be a mage thing?" He brought the water flask to her.

Daja drank gratefully. "Thank you. I don't know. There's plenty of mage things I never heard of."

"Where do you see it?"

She pointed to the open sea. "I keep thinking there's a ship out there, a plain old felucca—"

" 'A plain old'—what?"

Poor Kirel was a landsman. "A felucca. A small sailing ship with lateen—triangle—sails. There's plenty in the harbor—the commonest ships around, for fishing or courier service or small cargo loads. But whenever I look straight at *this* felucca, there's nothing."

"Are you sure you see it in the first place?" He shaded his eyes, examining the water between Summersea's islands and the hills of the Emel Peninsula.

"It's clear enough I know what kind of ship it is," she reminded him.

"Oh." For a moment Kirel gazed out to sea, thinking. Suddenly he looked around for their teacher. "Frostpine!"

The man waved and jogged back to them. "What is it?"

"I've been seeing an *azigazi* all day," Daja explained. "At least, I don't *think* it's real. It's a plain felucca, after all, no reason for me *not* to see one if it really exists. They're common to these waters. But every time I look straight at the thing, it's gone."

Frostpine's dark eyes flashed. "Sense for it, as you sense for the metal in the net. Cast your magic out to sea. If it's a real ship, it's got metal on it."

She tried. Closing her eyes, she listened, and smelled. All that came to her mind was seawater, restless, treacherous stuff ready to grab the unwary.

"It's just *water*," she told Frostpine, almost whining. She knew she sounded like a baby, but really, what did he expect? The sea was the sea, not metal!

"Ack," he muttered, "you're being difficult." Standing behind her, he reached around and clasped her hands in his. "Remember how Sandry was able to spin a magic cord from your inner self? Well, throw one out to me."

She tried to find the thread, but his touch was distracting her. It was easy to hand a cord to Sandry, who was giving and soft, like well-woven cloth. Frostpine, though, was metal from top to toe. His metal rang where it touched hers, or rattled. Not cord, then, but wire, she thought. Taking a deep breath, reaching inside, she drew out a shimmering wire and passed it to him.

"Good enough," he said. She felt his power bend, and spring. He towed her magic forward, intertwined with his. Now she felt metal pass under and beside her as their power flew outward: pieces of chain, a metal-bound chest, a discarded anchor, all of it rusting on the ocean floor. They slowed; Frostpine sprang forward again. Their power swept further out—

It *had* to be a ship. What else held nails and metal straps in quite that way, as if she saw a vessel stripped of its wood? Wincing, she realized that she saw weapons, too: a number of swords and knives that no innocent fishing boat should carry, and clusters of metal arrowheads.

Exhaling the breath in his own lungs, Frostpine ran back to the shore, taking Daja gently along. When she opened her eyes, she staggered.

Frostpine caught her. "You two load the pieces of net we've found, and bring them inside the walls," he ordered Kirel. "Don't dawdle. I'm telling them to close the gates."

Daja grabbed Frostpine's arm before he could go. "It's just one ship—"

He patted her cheek gently. "If his business were honest, youngster, he wouldn't be hidden, would he? That's a pirate's scout vessel, or I'm a dancing girl. Help Kirel, and come in with him."

"Even if it's a scout, the main pirate fleet's nowhere near, surely?" Picking up a stack of net-pieces, she loaded them into one of the mule's baskets.

"Not yet," Kirel replied, filling the other basket. "They might be waiting for dark."

"How long have you been sensing this *azigazi?*" Frostpine asked.

"Since—I don't know," Daja said, genuinely scared. Pirate tales had given her nightmares since she was a ground-pounding baby, too little to sail in the family ships. "It was at least an hour before midday."

"I'll wager they don't know we've spotted them. Don't look so frightened," Frostpine said with a grin. "You've given us warning, that's all. And next time, pay more attention to your *azigazis!*"

5

Once they'd eaten midday, Rosethorn gave Briar inside work, filling small bottles with different syrups and muslin bags with blends of dried herbs. While he got to work, Rosethorn showed Tris how to make a paste of the finely ground beef and hardboiled egg yolks Briar had carried up from the kitchens. Rolling the paste into tiny balls, Tris fed them to the nestling at the end of a thin bit of wood. The bird would get those, and a few drops of water, alternately with the milk-and-honey mixture. The dedicate also helped Tris set up a special burner, a metal box that held a candle, to heat small amounts of goat's milk and honey as they were needed. Once the rest period was over, Rosethorn decided that the nestling could be fed every half hour, instead of every fifteen minutes. Loading a basket with the bottles and bags that Briar had filled, she told him to prepare a bushel basket of willow bark strips for tea, and left.

Once she was gone, Tris went upstairs for some books she was supposed to be reading. She bundled her hair under a kerchief, shed her shoes and stockings, and returned to the workshop, prepared for a long afternoon. Rosethorn had set her up in front of a window that gave a good view of the Hub clock. Briar, tearing small pieces of bark to shreds, was close enough to be company without making Tris feel crowded. She felt relaxed for the first time in hours.

"She's not so bad, is she?" Briar asked when they'd been silent for a while. "I mean, she's not sweet, like Lark, but she has her good side."

"You must be the only person in all Winding Circle who would say that," remarked Tris drowsily. Taking off her spectacles, she leaned her hand on her chin, gazing out the window through half-lidded eyes. It was a relief not to have light flickering on the edges of her vision.

Did Niko see this way all the time? Didn't his eyes get tired? There was magic *everywhere* in Winding Circle, she'd found—in the south gate where it pierced the eight-foot-thick wall, in the stones of the spiral road through the temple community, in windows and doors. It blazed along the entire length of the Hub, and from the Water and Fire temples, and shone from the mages and their students she had passed. Most interesting, to her point of view, it gleamed throughout Discipline and blazed in this workshop—she wondered what she might see in Lark's workroom. All this time, she hadn't thought Lark and Rosethorn were as powerful as Niko, an acknowledged great mage. She had assumed that their magics were smaller, because they were centered around such ordinary things.

Maybe she needed to think again.

Soft cheeps came from the nest. Glancing at the clock, the girl realized that it was time to feed her charge. She placed her spectacles on her nose and took the cover from the nest.

"Ugly little peep," Briar remarked, watching over her shoulder as she dripped liquid into the gaping beak. "What're those spiky things?"

"Rosethorn says they're pinfeathers. Once he fledges—once he gets real feathers—he'll grow up pretty fast." Turning to find a wet cloth to mop up spilled milk, she was struck by a blaze of silver light that flared out from a fat, leather-bound book. Tris flinched, covering her eyes.

Hands steadied her on the stool. "Careful—you almost fell off. What's got into you, anyway? You've been a-flinch and a-twitch since you got back."

Tris sighed. Finding the cloth, she wiped away her mess and covered her charge. "Niko did this thing to my specs," she told him, and explained about her new ability to see magic. "It takes getting used to. I suppose I will, eventually. Niko doesn't twitch all the time."

"So—if you see this—light, is it?"

"Mostly it's like there's a silver veil over things, or they have silver marks. Then there are the ones that shine like lamps. *Big* ones. Like the Hub—and not just the seeing and hearing places. The whole tower, clock to kitchens."

"And all of that light's magic."

"That's what Niko told me."

Briar thought about this, tapping the countertop with a reed.

"You'll wake my bird." Tris took the reed away.

"We heard what you heard last night," Briar remarked abruptly.

"Yes." She looked up at him, waiting. He scowled, not liking the direction his thoughts took him in.

"So maybe, because Her Highness spun us together, we pick up each other's magic. And we don't always have to be close together for it to spread."

"Maybe." Tris realized what he was getting at. "You're seeing the lights, too? And you think it's my magic crossing over?"

"I see glitter all over the house, and some on my way back from the Hub," he explained. "Not strong

62

like it is for you. But—" He hesitated, scratching his head.

"Will you make me wait all *day?*" demanded Tris. "I have reading to do."

He shrugged and told her about the figure in the Hub stairwell. "I figured it was just one of the students, trying out a new spell. I'd want to play with an invisibility spell, if I had one."

Tris's smile was only a bit sour. "Even *you* couldn't eat *all* the food you'd steal from Gorse with a spell like that."

"I don't think I'd get away with it. Gorse knows whenever *anybody's* in that kitchen, no matter how mad it gets in there. Still, it'd be worth a try." After a moment he added, "It was just weird to be seeing anyone using that kind of spell at all. At least now I know what I saw."

"Sorry," replied Tris. "How was I to know Niko's spell was catching? Listen—you want to work on reading while you shred that bark?" She had begun to teach him how to read a few days before and was surprised to find how much she liked it.

Briar's response was good for her vanity. He promptly dragged his stool and his willow bark over, then fetched a big slate and a piece of chalk. "First letter," he said, perching on his stool.

She wrote A on the black slate.

"A. Air, all-heal, Astrel, alder, animal. Followed by B."

Tris chalked the letter in.

He grinned. "Briar! Also Bit, berry, balm, bayberry, basil. Next letter's C—"

"Sandry." A cup touched her lips; she drank, tasting water flavored with lemon peel. Taking a breath, she tried to blink away the spell-pattern, feeling giddy. She and Lark had eaten at midday and gone right back to work.

The cup pressed against her lips again. This time she took it in her hands and drank the water in quick sips. When it was empty, she placed it on the table among heaped billows of thin cloth.

Looking at her work, Sandry frowned. She could see what Lark meant about this kind of weaving. It was too loose in some places and too thick in others. There were gaps. She thrust her fingers through two of them and sighed.

"It won't matter, with bandages." Lark stood beside the girl. It had been she who had called Sandry from her weaving trance. "There's always a layer on top or under, to catch leaks. You need to rest now, though. You're scaring our helpers." Sandry looked around, but the novices were missing. "They just took a load to the storerooms."

Sandry's blue eyes met Lark's smiling brown ones. "*Do* I scare them?" she whispered, rusty-voiced.

"A little. It's not that important—novices always need toughening up before they take their vows. They have to get used to powerful workings sometime. And *you* have company." She pointed to the open door.

A man in a somber brown tunic and breeches stood there, stripping off riding gloves. The sun gleamed on his shaved head, throwing his fleshy face partly into shadow. His brown eyes were set deep over a hawklike nose and wide, firm mouth. Broad-shouldered, heavily muscled, he wore command like a cloak. Meeting Sandry's eyes, he moved into the room and smiled. The shadow was gone; from a powerful and threatening figure, he changed into a pleasant, middle-aged man.

Half stumbling—how long had she been work-ing?—she curtsied and smiled back. "Uncle, I'm sorry!" she greeted Duke Vedris, ruler of Emelan. "I didn't know you were here."

He walked over and kissed her cheeks, as she kissed his. "A brief visit only, to meet with Honored Moonstream about the watchtowers that exploded." His voice was soft and elegant, the kind that people would strain to hear. He nodded toward the heaps of linen. "You've been very busy."

"I'm helping Lark." She offered him a chair. "We have tea, or fruit juice, if you'd like some."

Smiling, he shook his head. "I'm full of tea from the Hub. In any case, I can only stay briefly—I must return home by dark. Dedicate, please, sit," he told Lark.

"Actually, I'm going to let you and Sandry visit in

private," Lark said, going to the door. "I hope you don't mind."

The duke nodded. Lark bowed—dedicates weren't required to kneel or curtsy to nobles—and left them.

Vedris reached over and tugged one of Sandry's braids lightly, teasing her. "I'm glad to see you've recovered from *your* experiences during the earthquake. From what you and Niko said in your letters, it was quite dramatic."

"It was dramatic enough, I suppose." Sandry shuddered. "I'm lucky my friends were with me."

"As they were fortunate that you were there," pointed out the duke. "And what kind of work is this you're doing?"

She explained, showing him the finished rolls of cloth waiting for transportation to a storeroom. The sheer amount still in the workshop startled her—and she knew that more had already been taken to storage. A little awed, she stared at her fingers. It was so *easy*. That didn't seem right: Since she was new to this, shouldn't it cost more, to order thread to weave itself? She glanced at Lark's work. Even done this way, Lark's cloth was tighter and finer than hers.

"What strange turns life takes," the duke murmured, rubbing his naked scalp as he examined Sandry's bandages. "My nephew and his wife were sweet, but I cannot deny they were totally useless." He held up a hand to cut off her protest. "My dear, they lived for their own pleasure, doing nothing to

66

help those whose work gave them the money to do so. *You*, on the other hand—I have a feeling that you may achieve enough in your lifetime to make up for the emptiness of theirs."

She agreed—that was the worst part. She just couldn't bring herself to say as much aloud. "Aren't you being awfully hard on them?"

"Of course I am," he replied, brown eyes gleaming with amusement. "I'm a mean old pirate chaser whose life's work is to be hard on others." He pinched the bridge of his nose and sighed. "I'm getting too old for this, Sandrilene."

She stared at him. Since she was little, she'd viewed her father's favorite uncle as a marble man who never aged or tired. It was unsettling to hear him admit to weariness. "Is everything all right? Apart from pulling things together after the quake?"

"We have more pirates about than usual. I'd have thought the merchants' screams would be audible all the way up here."

She smiled and was glad to see that he smiled back. "Have they reason to scream?"

"Only if they hear the same news as I do. The worst of the Battle Islands raiders, Pauha—she calls herself *Queen* Pauha—has talked a number of the lesser chiefs into sailing under her command. That's bad enough—she can muster quite a fleet that way. Worse, her brother Enahar has joined her. He is a mage, educated at the university where Niko studied.

67

Enahar might complicate things, if Pauha turns her eyes our way."

"Is she going to?" The thought of a pirate fleet—not just a handful of ships—with a really good mage along made her skin prickle.

"I hope not." He got to his feet and stretched. Sandry also rose. "I'm doing my best to make them go elsewhere. Most of Emelan's fleet is at sea, guarding the coast." He gave her a strong hug. "Not that *you* need to worry. Winding Circle has its own way to discourage unwelcome visitors—no one has breached these walls in four hundred years."

"And Summersea?" she asked, walking with him to the door. Outside, a mounted company of the Duke's Guard waited under some shady trees.

His eyes glinted frostily. "They'd do better to swallow a crested porcupine. That's why our port is the most popular in the Pebbled Sea—we are the safest of all." He kissed her cheeks. "Be well, Sandrilene. Once things calm down, we'll have you and your friends up to Duke's Citadel, and you can show them around."

She caught his sleeve as a young guardsman brought over his horse. "Take care of yourself, Uncle. Let your merchants scream in a courtyard where you can't hear them. The exercise will keep them young."

He threw back his head and laughed. "*That's* my favorite niece!"

His guardsmen grinned as the duke mounted up. He saluted her and led the company up the spiral road. Sandry waved for as long as she could see him.

"I'm impressed," Lark said quietly. She came up to put a comforting arm around Sandry's shoulders. "The word is that he doesn't really like many people, and I can see he loves you."

"He works so hard," whispered Sandry. "I wonder if they appreciate him." She sighed, and looked into Lark's kind face. "And are *we* back to work?"

"For a while longer," the dedicate replied. "We'll stop at suppertime. You don't feel the effect of spending all this magic now, but you will tomorrow."

Five minutes later, as they were about to start their magical weaving again, a winded novice half fell through their door.

"Excuse me," she gasped, "but has Duke Vedris come here yet? Moonstream wants him back right away!"

Lark frowned. "He's gone. He may be through the north gate by now."

"Oh, cowpox!" cried the runner. She raced off.

Sandry fiddled uneasily with her spools of linen thread.

"It may be nothing," Lark said. "If it's bad news, we'll hear soon enough."

She was right. Taking a breath, Sandry eased into her magic, and the weaving resumed.

By suppertime, Sandry and Tris were half-asleep, worn out. Briar focused on eating, silently going over the letters Tris had taught him. Daja was restless, thinking of that hidden ship and what it could mean. Her clan had lost people and ships to pirates. Lark, Niko, and Rosethorn, together at supper for the first time since the earthquake, discussed the gossip that Rosethorn had picked up while working at the Water Temple.

"Niko, this spell is giving me a headache," Tris complained when the adults fell silent. "Do I need to see magic *all* the time? Doesn't it give *you* a headache?"

For a moment Niko caught her eyes with his and held them. Tris's vision doubled, then tripled as her teacher glowed, then blazed. "Ow!" she cried, breaking free to cover her eyes with her arm. "Stop it! That's worse than the flicker!"

"That is what I see," he explained, smoothing his mustache as he often did when thinking. "You're adapting to the spell quite nicely. It's not just the edges of your vision anymore, is it? You're starting to see magic when you look directly at it."

"You almost *blinded* me," she grumbled, rubbing her eyes with her fists.

"If you don't like it, alter the spell. Try to change the intensity of what you see. Dim the magic's glow." The edges of his eyes crinkled in a hidden smile.

"But I don't know what you did to my specs," she argued. "I have to know what you did to fool with your spell."

"Probe it with magic. You have to start learning

how to pick apart the spells cast by strangers anyway—think of this as a necessary exercise."

"Something in your eyes is flickering?" asked Daja.

"At the edges," Briar said, a spoonful of rice halfway to his mouth. "Like ghosts, only when—"

"Or *azigazis*," murmured Daja. When they all looked at her, she told them not just what the word meant, but what she had seen that afternoon.

"They're sniffing around," Rosethorn said grimly when Daja finished. "Scavengers. Parasites."

"At least we'll be safe," Lark replied. "Better they should blunt their teeth on us, or on Summersea—again—than go after a village still digging itself out."

"The duke's got patrols all up and down the coasts," Sandry pointed out. "They'll run off any pirates."

The dedicates, Sandry, and Tris made the gods-circle on their chests to ward off trouble. Daja placed one fist on top of the other as if she climbed a rope, the way to ask help of the Trader god. Briar, about to spit on the floor to scare off luck-eaters, caught Rosethorn's eye on him and cleared his throat instead.

They were about to get up from the table when Little Bear started to bark. Someone knocked on the door frame as the pup ran forward to challenge him.

Rosethorn shaded her eyes, trying to see the visitor's face through the open door. With the light just beginning to fade, he was only a shadow. "Not

Frostpine—too short," she muttered, and got up to greet the stranger. Briar grabbed Little Bear, who was sometimes over-enthusiastic in his welcomes.

"I'm sorry—I was told I might find the mage Niklaren Goldeye here?" The polite voice was male and young. Tris frowned; it seemed familiar.

"You found him," Rosethorn said, ushering the newcomer across the main room. "Would you like something to drink? We're just finishing supper."

"Thank you, no," he said with a half smile. "I ate at the dining hall."

As the visitor came near, they could see he was a good-looking young man, with tumbled brown hair and lively, smiling eyes of the same color. His nose was long and arched, his mouth and chin determined. He wore the styles that Niko preferred, though Sandry could tell that this man was more interested in fashion. His red shirt was embroidered in white around the neck and down the front; his pale gray over-robe had very full sleeves. Niko's embroideries, when he had them, were often the same color as the material they were stitched on, while the sleeves of his robe only reached to his elbow, a style popular ten years before. The young man's loose breeches were a slightly darker gray than his robe, with a satin stripe along the outer leg-seams. He wore calf-high boots with a design of tiny mirrors set into the tops, and a gold hoop earring in one ear.

"Master Goldeye?" he asked Niko. "I come from

Lightsbridge. Adelghani Smokewind asked me to bring you a letter." He offered a folded and sealed parchment to Niko. Briar released Little Bear, now that he was calmer. The pup would have jumped up to paw at the visitor's chest, but instead the man half knelt and turned the dog into his motionless friend by scratching his rump.

"Smokewind?" asked Niko, breaking the seal on the parchment. "How was he? Does arthritis still trouble him?"

The visitor had a boy's open smile. "It makes him cross on damp days, sir. He tells students that if he's in pain, they must suffer with him."

Niko smiled. "Smokewind has always been good at sharing his moods."

Lark whispered to Daja, "Let's clear—" She glanced at Tris and frowned.

Tris stared at the newcomer as if he had two heads. Her face had gone white and pinched; her eyes were huge behind her spectacles. "C-cousin *Aymery?*" she whispered.

The young man looked at her. "Yes, Aymery's my name." To the adults he added, "I'm Aymery Glassfire, I should have said before—Glassfire is my mage name. But you, little girl—" He stopped speaking, and blinked several times. At last he cleared his throat and said, "It's Darra and Valden's girl, isn't it? The—the one who likes to read? Treze—Troi—Trisana, that's it."

She looked down, blushing. "Yes."

Now he frowned, puzzled. "The last time I was in Ninver—how long ago?"

"Two years," she whispered.

"That's right. And they'd sent you to live with Uncle Murris and Aunt Emmine. No one would tell me why."

Tris nodded.

Aymery looked from her to Niko. "I—I don't know what to say." There was an odd light in his eyes. "I never thought to find relatives here. I just promised Smokewind I'd give you that letter, since I was coming to Winding Circle."

Lark got up and beckoned to her chair. "Sit down, please. I think you really must stay a while, don't you? I'm Dedicate Lark, by the way."

Introductions were made. Tris, aware that everyone was now watching her, got up and began to clear the plates.

"You should be glad to see family," Daja murmured. She poured hot water into the tub they used to wash dishes. "You don't *look* happy."

"They got rid of me," retorted Tris softly, letting some plates ease into the tub.

"Was he part of it?" Sandry whispered, taking the hot water kettle from Daja. She yawned and nearly spilled its contents on the Trader's feet.

"No, he—" Tris looked back at the table.

Aymery was telling the dedicates and Niko, "I had

to use the library here for my studies. I'm almost finished with my mastery credential—"

"He left before they got rid of me for good," Tris said quietly, remembering. "That same fat toad that tested me for magic—"

"The one who said you didn't have any?" Briar asked, taking up a towel so he could dry the clean dishes.

"That one. He tested Aymery and said he ought to go to Lightsbridge. Usually Aymery visited for the winter holiday. Summer ones, too, for a while. The last time he was home at all was two years ago."

"He dresses like a Bag," Briar remarked. "I like his glitter." A tug of his fingers on his earlobe told the girls he meant Aymery's earring.

Tris turned her head sideways—it was still the best way to look for magic, on the edges of her sight. She didn't notice that her friends did the same thing. There was magic in Aymery, sure enough, a shift and glimmer of pale light twined around his core, as well as a bright spot on his earring. Aymery's magic was a pale moonglow, almost blotted out by the suns that blazed in Lark, Rosethorn, and Niko.

Did *she* glow? she wondered. Turning her head, she examined her friends. Did *they*? She thought she saw something in them, but it shifted and hid when she tried to pin it down.

"Tris," Rosethorn said. She pointed to her workshop: the nestling was calling. "This should be the last feeding of the day."

Hurriedly Tris poured the last of the goat's milk into a cup and carried it into the workshop. Once it was safely in the little pan, she put it on to heat. Her nestling was cheeping more loudly than he had that morning. That *has* to be a good thing, she thought, though at the moment it simply made her nervous. The milk seemed to take forever to warm, and she had almost forgotten honey. Running to the supper table, she grabbed the bowl and carried it back, to gently add a tiny spoonful to the heating liquid.

At last it was warm. She took the pan off the heat, stinging her fingers, then thrust in the reed and capped the dry end with her finger. Gently removing the handkerchief that sheltered her charge, she could see that he wanted to be fed, right now. Carefully she dripped milk into his yawning beak, until he'd had enough. Staring up at Tris, he burped, then settled down to sleep.

"You do that very well."

She twitched, getting a drop of milk on her cheek. Dabbing it off with a bit of cotton, she looked at her cousin. He leaned on the counter, his dark eyes serious. He was nearly twenty-two, she remembered, one of three boys and two girls in her uncle's family. He was their pride and joy, the future mage who would make them rich.

"I've been practicing all day." She covered the nest

carefully and blew out the candle that served as her cook-fire. With relief she saw that the sun had finally passed below the top of the outer wall.

"Why aren't you in Ninver?" he asked. "All Master Goldeye would say is that you're his student. I'm envious, you know. Niklaren Goldeye is on the Mage-Council of Lightsbridge. He's very famous."

"Will you stop talking long enough for a person to answer your questions?" she demanded.

He smiled, but there was something nervous in his eyes. "Sorry. I guess I'm excited, meeting him, and—and finding you, of course. Why are you here?"

"They didn't want me," she said flatly. "They gave me to Broken Circle Temple, and Broken Circle sent me here. I didn't know till I'd been here for weeks that Broken Circle sent me because I had magic."

"Do you mean the magic-seer didn't find it?" Aymery wasn't looking at her; instead he drew invisible signs on the countertop. "He saw it in *me*."

"Not me," she said, her temper starting to heat. "The family, and Broken Circle—they thought I was possessed, or haunted, or—not all human. They—" Bundles of herbs drying overhead rustled. Leaves on the floor whipped, shaken by the rising wind.

Tris glared up into her cousin's face. Now that she thought of it, Aymery—whose eyes always looked as if they smiled just for the person he looked at, even when the person he looked at had been *her*—Aymery had always been kind. He'd never done her any harm.

Tris sighed and let go of the rage that had been growing in her throat. Leaves dropped back to the floor. Herbs settled, their fragrance drifting around the room. "Niko says my magic's—strange. It's tied into weather. I don't understand it myself."

Aymery shook his head. "They *told* us a mage never stops learning new things. Ah—Trisana—"

"Tris," she said. "Only Cousin Uraelle called me by my full name."

"Tris. I had a letter from Mother—it was waiting for me when I got here. She says Uncle Valden is ill, maybe dying. I think you should go home, as soon as possible."

She blinked at him. How on earth was she supposed to feel about news like this? "If my father wants me, he'll send for me," she snapped. Herbs rattled overhead, harder than a moment ago; leaves and dust twirled on the floor. Breezes plucked at their hair and clothes. "The last time I saw him, he told a stranger that he and my mother didn't want me back. Not ever!"

"You can't let that stand in your way," Aymery insisted. "Go home while you can—that's what *I'd* do. Go home, now, and make your peace with him. I'll give you money for your passage. And there's a ship in Summersea—"

The herbs were now flapping in the air, tossed by the rising wind in the little room. One bunch snapped from its mooring and flew through the door into the main room.

"Tris," Niko called in a warning voice.

Briar leaned into the door, the bunch of herbs in one hand. "Get hold of yourself!" the boy hissed. "If you make a mess after all the straightening I did—"

"What is it? What's the matter?" Aymery wanted to know, looking from Briar to the blushing Tris.

She knew what it was. She'd started to lose her temper again, heating up the air around her. If she didn't calm down, she could start a whirlwind in here—small thanks for all Rosethorn's kindnesses today. Taking a deep breath, she folded her hands before her and counted, slowly, thinking only of her breath and the numbers.

The air in the workshop went still.

"Master Niko! Master Niko!" shouted someone from the front of the cottage. "You're needed at the Hub!"

Tris and Aymery followed Briar into the main room. Everyone was staring at the disheveled novice who clung to the door frame, panting.

"What's wrong?" asked Niko, rising from his seat.

"You won't believe it," gasped the novice. "It happened, it happened just a few minutes ago. Every crystal and mirror in the seeing-room shattered. Every one! Even the water bowls where people look for visions broke!"

Niko left the cottage at a run.

"But that's impossible, isn't it?" Rosethorn asked Lark nervously. "The Hub is spelled for protection, inside and out."

"A tremor in the earth?" suggested Aymery. Tris, standing close to him, noticed that his hands were shaking.

"None of the mirrors or crystals so much as cracked during the earthquake," Lark said. "Not a one."

Aymery sighed. "Well! I'd only be in the way, if I offered to help. I may as well go to the library and start my research. May I claim a kiss, cousin?"

Tris scowled at him. Undaunted, Aymery kissed her on the cheek. "You should go home," he whispered. He thanked the women and left.

Lark remained at the door, staring unhappily at the Hub. "What could do this?" she whispered. "It leaves us blind to whatever the future throws at us. Haven't we had enough surprises for one summer?"

It was not even three in the morning when Tris opened her eyes. Something was wrong with the air. The winds that usually blew across Winding Circle from the north at this hour were turning, coming back when they should have been headed out to sea. She felt as if a heavy animal paced overhead, pressing her down, making it hard to breathe.

Her starling was asleep and shouldn't wake until dawn. That was still a good two hours away.

Somehow she dressed, bundled her hair under a kerchief, and stumbled out of the cottage. Little Bear followed her to the southern wall and up the stairs.

For Tris, climbing was agony to legs that still ached from the long hike to the Bit Island tower. She gritted her teeth and kept moving, trying not to trip on her skirts or the dog. Once atop the wall, she found the spot where the four had been the night before and peered out to sea.

The strangely baffled wind twitched around her like a bad omen. Above the Circle to the north, it was a fine night, with no clouds to veil the stars or the thin sliver of the moon. On her right, the glow of the Maja beacon shone over the dark hump of Bit Island. The peninsula on her left was dark with the Pirate's Point watchtower gone.

Directly ahead, over a mile out to sea, a storm waited, its masses of towering clouds flickering with lightning. Sheets of rain kept her from seeing any distance into it. It stretched in a broad, heavy band as far to the west and the east as Tris could see, moving slowly on the harbor islands and down the peninsula.

She frowned. The land breezes should have been sucked right into the thing, feeding it. Instead they stopped at its leading edge, as if they had struck a wall. Tugging the tip of her nose, she turned her head slightly. Everywhere that cloud masses touched the side of her vision, silver light blazed.

Tris shut her eyes and inhaled, creating stillness within. Her mind leaped free of her body, grabbing air as it rushed by. Down she spilled, riding the wind as it flowed over the torn ground leading from the south gate to the sea. She sped along the water, foam-topped waves tickling her belly. Soaring up, she dove in—

And slammed into a glass-smooth wall. Hissing in fury, the wind/Tris thumped the obstacle and raced back to shore. Finding a stronger gust, she rode it straight at the mass, to smash into its glassy front. She skidded up its length, expecting to slide a long way: true storm clouds would rise at least three miles into the air. Instead, at a most unstormlike height of less than a mile, she zipped over a hump of some kind. She slid over the hard roof on the mass for two miles or so, feeling no breaks or entrances under her. Riding with her fellow breezes, unable to drop to the sea and get comfortable, she circled, balked as a cat who'd just lost a mouse. Her trip back to shore was shorter by a hair than the trip out. The thing, whatever it was, was rolling forward slowly. When it reached the land, would it tell her where she could blow there, too?

A dog's shrill yapping broke her concentration. Tris was jerked from the wind back into her own mind.

"You again. Look—you shouldn't *be* here." It was the tall, thin guard of the night before. His partner stood nearby, a crossbow in one hand, Little Bear's collar in the other. The pup barked and struggled to get free. "A pirate scout was reported in the cove this afternoon," the man continued. Tonight the guards wore battle gear: helmets and leather jerkins studded with metal rings, scarlet tunics that fell to mid-thigh, and heavy sandals. "No visitors allowed. And can't you make your dog shut up?"

"No," said Tris flatly. She pointed at the storm. "Does that look normal to you?"

"It's a *storm*," replied the woman guard. "We could use the rain."

"If that's a storm, then I'm Duke Vedris," snapped Tris. "Storm clouds reach up for *miles*. These aren't high enough even for an afternoon squall!"

The guards traded looks.

"Am I a mage or am I not?" yelled Tris. Puffs of wind teased her hair, tugging the kerchief from her head and sending it flying off the wall. "Last night I was a mage, and so were my friends. Now, either I'm a mage and you ought to listen to me, or you handled us wrong last night. Which is it?"

"It won't hurt to let the captain know what she says," the woman remarked slowly. "I don't know much about storms."

"I do!" said Tris. The wind yanked not only at her clothes, but at the guards'. Taking deep breaths, she fought to control her temper. This was no time to see how strong a wind it would take to knock her into the cove. "Will you *please* listen to me?"

Abruptly the man turned and trotted down the wall, bound for one of the stout round towers that flanked the south gate. When he returned, another man—shorter, stockier, black-skinned—came with him. Tris repeated what she'd told the guards to the newcomer, who raised a long metal tube to one eye and pointed it toward the storm.

"She's right." He lowered the tube. "That's no real storm. You—"

"Tris," she supplied, when she realized what he waited for.

"Tris. Good work. Now, take your dog and go back to bed. We'll have the warrior-mages out here in no time."

Breathing easier now that someone believed her, Tris took Little Bear and went home.

"Daja," a male voice said in her ear. "Daja, wake up."

"Go 'way, Uneny." Asleep, she thought it was her older brother, that she was in her hammock on Third Ship Kisubo. "I'm not takin' your watch."

"Daja, it's Frostpine. I need you."

She sat up, planning to box Uneny's ears.

Her bedside candle was lit. She was in a landsman's house, on a standing bed. From the corner, the god-statues of Trader Koma and Bookkeeper Oti shimmered in the flickering light of her candle. She blinked at her teacher. "Frostpine?"

"We have work to do. Get dressed." He put a steaming bowl into her hands and left.

The bowl was filled with hot chocolate, a rare and expensive drink served only on important occasions. Impressed, she put on her clothes, sipping the sweetened liquid. By the time she padded downstairs, she was wide awake. Glancing out an attic window, she saw by the Hub clock that it was just after five in the morning.

Lark and Rosethorn were seated at the kitchen table, looking bleary-eyed. Even Little Bear, who liked to bark as everyone got up in the morning, was sprawled before the cottage altar, fast asleep. Frostpine, pacing the floor, smiled as Daja reached the bottom of the stairs.

"Sit." He gently pushed her onto a stool by the table. "Are you awake?"

Daja nodded as she finished buttoning a red gauze shirt.

"Good. Listen to me: I've been asked to do something dangerous." Crouching before her, he gathered her hands in his. "There's a masking spell stretched from the Emel Peninsula east, past Astrel Island and Duke's Citadel. We're nearly certain it's covering a large pirate fleet. His Grace wants me to renew and strengthen the spells on the chain that blocks the harbor mouth *now*, which means working right under the pirates' noses. I could use your help, but only if you understand the risks. We'll be covered by powerful magical shields, but it's one thing to know you're safe in your *mind*, and another to know it in your belly."

"Think about this, Daja," Lark said, her usually cheerful voice husky with sleep and worry. "You'll be in a boat—you won't be able to run away if the fleet attacks. You won't be able to change your mind once you're out there."

Daja looked into Frostpine's bright, dark eyes. "What kind of shields do we have?"

"A chunk of the spell-net we dug up yesterday. *Think* about this a minute, girl. I'll die before I'll let anything happen to you, but if you're afraid, I want to know it now."

She stared through the open door to Lark's workroom. A year ago, Third Ship Kisubo was about to put to sea out of Hajur when Fifth Ship Kisubo limped into the harbor. She had just survived a pirate attack with tattered sails and a charred aftercastle. One mast had been sheared off in the middle. When they lowered the gangplank—when the crew of Third Ship Kisubo had gathered on the dock to help—the first one to disembark from Fifth Ship was Uncle Tiwolu. His sweat-streaked ebony face was sorrow-twisted. In his arms he carried the bloody corpse of Aunt Zayda, the ship's captain, riddled with *jishen* arrows.

Taking a deep breath, Daja nodded. "I'll do it."

Rising, Frostpine tugged her to her feet. "Let's go." He took a haversack from the table and slung it onto his back. "Our escort's waiting outside."

Daja kissed Lark on the cheek, then looked at Rosethorn. The auburn-haired dedicate glared at her. "There's no need to get emotional," she informed Daja tartly. "I'll see you in a few hours."

Daja grinned. She had expected no other response from Rosethorn. "In a few hours," she promised, and followed Frostpine out of the cottage. A ten-squad of the Duke's Guard, armored in black leather jerkins and helmets stitched with black-enameled metal rings, waited for them. One of them held the reins of a riderless horse; the rest were already mounted.

"She's with you?" The speaker was a short, stocky woman with the twin yellow arrowheads that marked her as a sergeant on her helmet.

Frostpine nodded and swung himself into the saddle, distributing his habit so it didn't get twisted under him. He then reached an arm down to Daja. When she grabbed it, he lifted her up behind him, ignoring her squeak of dismay. She found her bottom was resting on a hard roll of cloth. "You've got my pack?" Frostpine asked the man next to them. The soldier patted one of his saddlebags.

"North gate," the sergeant ordered, and nudged her steed into motion. As Frostpine's horse lurched under them, Daja cringed and wrapped both arms around her teacher's waist. When they switched to a trot, Daja buried her face in Frostpine's habit and prayed to Koma, for protection from pirates, and to her ancestors, for protection from land-perils like horseback riding. She only knew they had passed through the north gate by the clanging echo of hooves in the tunnel through the wall.

"Listen to me," Frostpine said quietly. "Are you listening?"

"Yes," Daja replied. "I'm just not looking."

"You don't need to look. Here's our plan. You'll sense for weakness in the metal—do you remember how?"

"Yes." She had learned that earlier in the summer.

"Once we're at the chain—it's two chains, actually—our boat will take us along it link by link, from the Tombstone to the Harbormaster's tower," Frostpine went on. "If you find a weak spot, tell me—even if it seems unimportant. I'll strengthen it as I strengthen the spells on the chain." Reaching back, he patted her knee. "I wish I didn't have to do this with you, but—"

"I'm the only other one with smith-magic at Winding Circle." She took her face out of his clothes so he could hear her soft voice. "I'm the only one who can feel things like you do."

"If things go wrong, I may need to draw on your power," he added. "It may take both of us to finish the job."

"*Serious* magic," breathed Daja.

"As serious as anything you *or* I have ever done."

When they turned off the road to Summersea to follow a steep track downhill to the harbor, Daja hid her face again. Finally they stopped; she could hear the welcome sound of waves slapping rock. When

Frostpine dismounted, she opened her eyes to see they were on the southeast side of Bit Island, inside the harbor wall. Torches had been planted in the sand to cast light on a waiting longboat, crewed by men and women in the dun jerkins and breeches of the ducal navy. Daja slid off the horse and ran for the boat, blushing crimson at the soldiers' laughs. Once aboard, she planted herself quite solidly on the middle bench.

"We need to work on your riding," Frostpine remarked as he pulled the hard cloth bundle off his horse.

"We need do no such thing," she muttered in Tradertalk. "I'll just walk."

"Walking carries no freight, and a freightless Trader is a poor one," he replied in the same language, opening the cloth. From it he drew a long roll of silvery mesh. Its mirrors and wire glinted in the torchlight.

Carefully the guards climbed into the longboat. Five had brought long spears. They seated themselves among the sailors and braced their weapons between their knees and feet. Once they were settled, Frostpine passed the metal net aboard the boat. The sailors opened it to its full length and width, then fastened it overhead, using the spears to hold it like a canopy. Once it was secure, other guards took crossbows and quivers from their saddles and boarded, leaving one of their number to look after their mounts.

Daja was shifted to the port rail, one bench away from the prow. Frostpine was on the same side, two benches behind her, the pack that a guard had carried for him between his knees. When everyone was in place, the guards with spears angled them outward, stretching the metal net canopy until it covered the boat.

"I won't activate the spell until we're at the chain," Frostpine told everyone. "But keep this in mind: once I have, *don't look overhead*. It would prove very unsettling, take my word for it."

Daja nodded hard. She could vouch for how unsettling the spell-net could be!

"Once we're in sight of the chain, no talking except in whispers," ordered the sergeant, placing her crossbow on her lap. "And be miserly with those!" Everyone nodded. Living near the sea all their lives, they knew how sound carried over open water.

The coxswain nodded to the pair of sailors who stood outside the boat, ankle-deep in the gentle harbor surf. Grunting, they pushed the boat into deeper water and hopped in. The coxswain whistled softly, and the oars went up; a second whistle, and they bit into the water.

Daja felt better already.

Bit and Crescent Islands passed on the left like shadows. Seeing trees on the islands, Daja realized that it was almost fully light. She huddled down, feeling uncomfortably visible, even with the bulk of the island and the thick harbor wall between them and the menace at sea. There were no glimpses of it to be had; the wall kept it from view.

When they hit larger waves off Maja Island, a strained voice said, "How much longer?"

It was Frostpine. A sailor hooked a hand through the belt on his habit, allowing the dedicate to lean over the side. Taking deep breaths, Frostpine locked one hand on the bench, the other on the rail, gripping them so hard that his knuckles turned white.

Daja had a smile under her hand. "I'd've thought you sailed better," she whispered.

"I don't. I need faults, to accent my excellence—otherwise—" He gulped. "I would be too wonderful to live with." He gasped and made a dreadful noise deep in his throat.

"Lucky girl, to have so modest a teacher," joked a guard softly.

"He thinks it's bad now," the sergeant whispered, grinning. "He ought to be *outside* the harbor. That's where the *real* sea beats. This here is like boating in my washtub."

They came out to Maja Island's lee. Ahead in the gray morning light was the harbor's mouth, an opening fifteen hundred yards wide. On the west it was guarded by the rising bulk of the Harbormaster's tower, on the east by the granite lump and smaller tower of the Tombstone. Beyond them, lightning flickered against a mass of black clouds.

Daja gasped.

"It's a fake," the coxswain told her, clipped voice mild. "Mage-work."

Daja tried to relax. If it was a fake, it was a *convincing* fake of a ship-killer storm.

Something at the foot of the Harbormaster's tower flickered in the corner of her eye. She frowned and made herself look dead ahead. There, in her side vision, a galley-shaped billow of silvery fire rocked in the lee of the huge tower, inside the wall. Another such shape—a galley spelled to invisibility—lay off the Tombstone. These had to be the duke's ships, Daja realized, shielded by magic and serving as an extra, secret guard at the harbor mouth. It wasn't just the enemy outside who believed in hiding in plain sight.

Carefully rising, Frostpine touched the net and hummed a snatch of music. Daja looked away as white fire rippled along the strands of the metal web, calling its many embedded spells to life. A soldier moaned; he'd looked at their canopy. A sailor reached out and yanked his chin, forcing him to take his eyes from it.

Quietly, oars barely splashing, they coasted to the mouth of the harbor. The chain, hidden far below in peacetime, was up.

Daja sighed with admiration. Calling the thing across the entrance a chain was misleading. It resembled a ladder. A pair of chains thirty feet apart formed the sides, and whole logs formed its rungs. The chains were fastened to metal collars on the logs to keep the metal links out of the sea. The ends of the logs were sharp points. Any ship that tried to break the chain would ram itself. And even if a ship somehow broke one of the metal strands, the other would still hold the logs together.

"It's *beautiful*," she whispered. Brown eyes glowing, she looked around at the mute granite of the Tombstone and at the huge, solid Harbormaster's tower. From there her gaze moved to the broad stone wall that stretched from the Harbormaster's to Astrel Island, just like the walls that connected Astrel to the Arsenal and those that connected the eastern harbor islands. "No wonder this is the safest anchorage on the Pebbled Sea."

"Nice and homelike," quipped a seaman in a whisper.

"Bows," came the sergeant's hushed command. The soldiers readied their crossbows, sliding bolts into the notches.

Daja watched the storm. Now she could see the thing was motionless, dead in the water. The lightning that flashed over its long front followed the same tracks, time after time, each ripple and jag the same. Any lingering fear she had that this was a real storm dried up.

As they drew close to the double chain, Daja shivered with awe. Each iron link was two inches thick, nearly a foot long, and inlaid with spell-letters in different metals, each of them a magical working to prevent rust, breakage, trickery, or accident. In its way, it was every bit as complicated and thorough as the spell-net. This was magic of the oldest and strongest kind. If I study for *years*, she thought, will I have a tenth of the knowledge it took to create these things?

Frostpine rummaged in the pack. He drew out a bottle of oil, breaking the seal on the cork.

"We brought no boathooks," whispered the coxswain. "How do we pass under the inside chain—?"

Daja looked back at her teacher. Frostpine held a finger to his lips, and signaled for the oarsmen to bring them up to the first length of metal. When they were just a few feet away, Frostpine closed his eyes and smiled.

She wasn't sure that the seamen felt it, but *she* did: a thin shiver in the air. Someone gasped. The immense metal links that lay between them and the outer chain rose into the air: a yard, two yards. They ghosted under it, oars flat to their sides—no one dared look up to see if their canopy so much as touched it. Daja heard a clink of metal as the chain lowered itself again.

Frostpine sighed. When she looked back, he was rubbing oil into his hands. Pointing to the outer chain, he made shooing motions at Daja: she was to get to work. Once she was within reach, Daja leaned forward and grasped the first oversized link. With a deep breath, she cleared her mind of questions and let her magic flow. Link by link she explored the metal between the Tombstone and the first log, hunting for any crack or speck of rust that would make it shatter if the enemy tried to ram it.

Her power reached as far as the first log. Glancing back at Frostpine, she nodded. His wrists and hands gleamed with the powerfully scented oil from his bottle. She'd seen him make it several days ago for use on the metal fittings of the temple gates. A mixture of rosemary, rose geranium, and cypress oils, it was steeped in protective spells. It cast a magical glow in her mind that warmed her and made her feel brave.

Frostpine went over the chain that she had just checked, rubbing oiled hands over every link. When they reached the first log, the oarsmen rowed them back to the inner chain. As they approached, it rose again, lowering itself once they were through. When it was back in place, Daja examined it with her own magic, and Frostpine followed her power with his. Once that section was done, the sailors rowed them around the first log and brought them back to the inner chain, where they did it all again.

They were a third of the way across when someone poked her shoulder and pointed. Still within her own magic, Daja looked at the stalled mass of the illusion-storm. Two strange boxes bobbed in the water before it, one on a course that led straight to their boat, the other a thousand feet away, bound for the

Harbormaster's massive tower. They were wood, painted dead black. Something about them made Daja feel very nervous. There was a gleam of spell-letters written under that paint. She didn't like the way that, every time she tried to give the nearest one a good look, her vision skittered off it like a raindrop on glass. And wasn't that a familiar sensation? One from an *azigazi* the day before, perhaps?

"Debris from what's on the other side?" suggested the coxswain.

"They go against the current," whispered a soldier. "Movin' right at us, too."

"Coming at the chain. That's what it wants." The sergeant's voice was barely audible.

"Daja," murmured Frostpine, "breathe in. Deep breath. Deep, *deep* breath. You're—a bellows. Blow that thing away from us."

A bellows?

Well, if Frostpine said she could be it, then she would. Those boxes might be harmless, but she didn't think so.

She thought of the bellows in his forge. It was so easy to handle that even a child could pump up enough of a blaze to melt iron. She breathed in. Her lungs were that powerful, able to draw in air and force it out with the strength of the gale. Her ribs were the metal fittings. All around she felt the warmth of the forge. Open, open, open, she thought as heat flooded her veins. The magic was in her, the magic of the forge. It had taken her over while she worked on the chain, with Frostpine so strong behind her. It had taken her, and now she would work it like hot gold.

Daja leaned over the side, not realizing a guard clutched her waistband to keep her aboard. One last little breath and *blow*, slow and strong, sending a hard stream of air at the box. It fought her, the puny thing, just like it fought the current, trying to keep to its course.

An oily hand gripped her shoulder: Frostpine had moved up right behind her. She forgot herself, forgot the danger, as her nose filled with the sharp scents of rosemary, rose geranium, and cypress. She filled her lungs with magic.

Leaning forward again, she clamped her chest muscles down hard and fast, slamming the magic out.

The box snapped from its course like a pit from a cherry, flying across over a thousand feet of sea to strike its mate. Both spun crazily in the water. As the guard and Frostpine pulled her back, the boxes thumped against the curved stone base of the Harbormaster's tower.

They vanished in a fireball. An invisible hand pressed them down, pressing the water with them. Something leaned on her eyes and ears. A thundering roar flashed through every bone she had. Caught between the logs of the chain, they might have been driven into them or crushed. Daja blew hard, staying a bellows long enough to keep them from being smashed. A shower of rock splinters and water fell through the spell-net canopy, cutting and drenching them. A splinter opened the skin on her right cheek.

When the smoke began to clear, she saw that some force had taken a giant bite from the curved base of the Harbormaster's tower.

In her mind, Tris, Sandry, and Briar were suddenly awake and clamoring. *What—? Daja, where—?*

Not now! she snapped. Outside the harbor the illusion-storm shivered. Light rippled all across its dark edges.

"I need to work through you," Frostpine told Daja hurriedly. "May I? I don't believe we should stay much longer."

The storm clouds were fading. Daja nodded to her teacher. "Do what you must."

Oily hands gripped hers. White fire raced through her bones, knocking her head back on her neck. Magic blazed around student and teacher in a widening arc, until it struck both chains. Down the chains the power raced, making them blaze. Daja would have screamed by then; she knew Frostpine would have screamed, but their throats had locked tight.

Someone poured a canteen full of water on them.

Gasping, teacher and student let go of each other.

"You can stop," the sergeant rasped, putting her

head close to theirs. "The whole thing's shining like noon at midnight. Get us out of here," she ordered the coxswain.

Daja tried to gasp quietly. An ugly headache was starting to hammer the back of her skull. Looking at Frostpine, she could see he was not much better off than she was.

But the sergeant was right. Both strands of the harbor chain shone as if made of lightning. From the concealed naval ships beside the harbor entrance, she heard cheering.

Staring through the blaze across the entrance, as she might stare into a forge-fire to see if her metal was hot enough, Daja gulped. The illusion-storm was gone. A hundred yards from the outer chain lay rank after rank of ships, large and small, flying a blood-red banner.

On the decks of two ships in the front line, Daja saw crews working to arm catapults. "But they can't see us," she whispered.

"They're aiming at something," a soldier pointed out.

"Row for your *lives*, damn you!" the coxswain snarled. No one was bothering to be quiet now.

The catapults loosed. From their cradles flew two round black balls, one at the Harbormaster's tower, one at the Tombstone. Each struck with a flash and a roar, followed by smoke, pressure, and rock splinters. She couldn't see what happened to the one that hit the Tombstone. The other ball had missed its target. Instead it struck the invisible ship on the Harbormaster's far side. The ship was visible now, with a vast hole in its deck, dead sailors everywhere, and flames shooting out of the hold.

Sandry turned over in bed and peeked at her front window. The sky was pearl gray—dawn was not far off. With a sigh, she burrowed deep into her pillow. The bells of the clock tower would clamor soon, but there was no harm in *trying* to get a little more sleep. . . .

The air around her *roared*. Yellow flashes and roiling gray smoke filled her eyes; a strange odor, bitter and clingy, invaded her nose. There was pressure on her face, as if someone leaned on a pillow fitted over her eyes and cheeks. Tiny, hard things sprayed her. A line of pain scored her right cheekbone.

Gasping, she sat up. There was a loud thud in the attic, as if Tris had fallen out of bed. Across the main room, through Briar's open door, she heard a flurry of curses.

What—? Daja, where—? all three clamored, speaking together in their minds.

Not now! came a sharp reply. Daja, it seemed, had other things to do just then. As if she cut it with scissors, the line connecting them to her snapped.

Sandry's nose prickled. She sneezed once, twice, and groped for her pocket handkerchief. Her eyes cleared. There was no smoke or fire in the room.

Scrambling out of bed, she ran to Briar's room. "Did you *feel* that?" she demanded.

He crawled out of what she called his nest, a mattress on the floor covered with a tangle of sheets. When he looked up at her, Sandry touched her scratched cheek: Briar sported a red weal at the identical spot. He frowned. "You, too?"

"What is going on here?" demanded Rosethorn, marching in. "Can't you three even get out of bed quietly?"

"Didn't you *hear* it?" Briar cried. "That—that *boom*, with the smell and the smoke!" He rubbed his eyes. "It pressed my head!"

Rosethorn's fine brows slanted down in a scowl. "I heard a boom, yes. I didn't *feel* a thing."

"Something happened to Daja," Sandry told her. "Where is she?"

"She and Frostpine went out an hour ago," snapped Rosethorn. "And *I* had just gone back to sleep."

"What's the ruckus?" Lark inquired from her room.

"They think something happened to Daja," called Rosethorn.

"She's all right," Briar said. "But something big's happening, and she cut us off."

Sandry had an idea. Returning to her room, she went to the shelf on which she kept her green spindle. Next to it was a circle of thread with four equally spaced lumps in it. During the recent earthquake, she had fixed her power and that of her friends to this thread, spinning magics like wool or silk, making them stronger. When they were done, the thread had become a circle. Now she picked it up, closed her eyes, and ran her fingers over the lumps, stopping at the one that cast the image of a forge-fire in her mind. She strained to enter the lump, Daja's knot, knowing it should help her to see what was happening to her friend. The power was there, but the images it made in her mind were ghosts that vanished before she knew what they were.

"Briar?" she called, without opening her eyes. "Tris?"

"How did she know I was out here?" grumbled Tris.

"I think they heard you crash down the steps at the Hub," Rosethorn said drily.

A rough hand closed over the one in which Sandry cupped Daja's thread-lump. Green light played over the inside of Sandry's eyelids. "What are we doing?" asked Briar.

"I think we can talk to Daja, or at least know what's going on. We just need to *reach*—"

He fed his magic into hers without a thought. It was far easier than something normal like going to sleep, which for Briar always meant triple-checks of hidden weapons, one more pat for the miniature tree on his windowsill, a check of the food stashed under his pillow and in his clothes chest. His magic *wanted* to combine with Sandry's. Intertwined, they strained, reaching along a thread of light that led toward a distant copper sun—and fell short.

A third, small, nail-bitten hand was laid over his and Sandry's. With Tris they weren't reaching. They were *there*, inside the copper blaze that was Daja in this use of their power. Now they saw as vividly through her eyes as they saw through their own.

Ranks of ships—war-galleys and smaller fighting craft—under a blood-red banner, were ranged behind a double chain that shone like white fire. Two round black balls arced up and away from catapults, one targeted on the Harbormaster's tower, the other against the Tombstone. Each struck: flashes, roars, smoke. There was no way to see where the one aimed at the Tombstone's watchtower hit. The other ball missed the Harbormaster's tower, dropping behind to hit something.

The roar, the flash: a wargalley that flew the banner of the Emelan dukes appeared, its invisibility gone. Its crew was screaming: a vast, fiery hole bloomed in its deck, and there were bodies everywhere.

Horrified, the three at Winding Circle yanked out of their joined hold. Sandry and Briar stared at each other with wide, frightened eyes. Tris swallowed hard, her face gray-green. Shouldering past Lark and Rosethorn in the doorway, she ran out the back.

Lark helped the pale, trembling Sandry to a seat. Briar sagged against the wall, rubbing his face. Rosethorn went out and returned with two cups of water. She handed one to Lark for Sandry, the other to Briar. He accepted it with a shaky smile and drank it dry. Smiling crookedly, she ruffled his hair.

"What happened to Tris?" asked Lark.

"We had a vision—a bad one. I don't think she's ever seen anyone killed before," Sandry explained after a few mouthfuls of liquid.

"At least, not all ripped to pieces." Briar shook his head.

"And you have?" Rosethorn asked, half smiling.

The smile vanished when his gray-green eyes met hers. "The Thief-Lord caught some kids that broke into his treasury once." Briar cleared his throat, feeling as if he'd inhaled strange, unpleasant smoke. "But this was a weapon, I think. What kind of weapon *does* that?"

"Could you tell us what you saw?" Lark suggested. "Rosie and I are a bit in the dark, still."

By the time they had finished describing what Daja had seen, Tris had returned. Everyone moved into the main room, taking seats around the table.

"Did you make it to the privy?" Rosethorn asked, getting some water for Tris.

The girl wiped her sweaty face on her nightgown sleeve. "Just," she admitted, drinking half of the water. Taking off her glasses, she poured the rest over her head. "Was that battlefire?" she asked, running her fingers through her tangled curls. "I thought battlefire was like jelly and just burned."

"It doesn't *sound* like battlefire," admitted Lark. "Had Daja ever seen this before?"

Looking at each other, the three children shook their heads.

"So it's pirates after all," Rosethorn said with a sigh. "And some new weapon. Time to start putting up burn ointments and wound cures."

"If they're at the harbor, they won't come here," protested Sandry. "Will they?"

"Even if they don't come here—and they haven't in recent memory," explained Rosethorn, "medicines are needed for those who have to fight. If they break through the harbor defense . . ."

The females drew the gods-circle on their chests. Briar hesitated, then did the same. He didn't think

Lakik the Trickster and Urda would mind if he called on bigger gods for protection at a time like this.

When the dawn bell began to ring, they all jumped. Just as they were relaxing, they realized the bell was ringing triple strikes for each normal, single chime.

Lark and Rosethorn glanced at each other. "They're calling in the outlying farms and villages," Rosethorn said.

"Is that bad?" Tris wanted to know.

Rosethorn shook her head. "Not if there are pirates off Summersea." Seeing the question in the children's faces, she sighed. "The harbor has resisted a great many attacks. I suppose pirates always think *they'll* be the ones to break into it, but often they just bottle up the entrances, so no one can go for help and so the fleet can't get out. What they *usually* do is land farther out, to go for the farms and villages outside the city walls and Winding Circle. We can't save the buildings, but we take in a great many people and animals."

"Here?" Tris wanted to know, dismayed. "At *Discipline?*"

"Relax," Lark told her. "The only time locals will stay here is if no young mages are living with us. They know youngsters aren't always in control of their power."

"Well, *that's* something, anyway," muttered Briar.

"My bird," said Tris, and ran upstairs.

108

"How do you feel?" Lark asked Sandry, examining her eyes and pressing her wrist to the girl's forehead. "I can't believe you were able to work magic this soon."

"I didn't work it very well," Sandry pointed out. "I needed Briar and Tris."

Rosethorn got to her feet. Gripping Briar's ear, she drew him along with her. "Come on, you," she ordered. "We'll set out breakfast."

"Rest your palms on mine," Lark told her student.

Sandry obeyed and closed her eyes. She felt something draw along her inner self, as if Lark teased a thread from a clump of wool. That bit of her tried to follow Lark's call, stretching.

"You're much stronger today than I expected," Lark said at last.

"I felt awful, before we tried to see what was wrong with Daja," admitted Sandry. "All wobble-kneed. My bones felt like overcooked noodles."

"We did a powerful lot of work yesterday—nearly three hundred yards of linen between us. You should be limp today." Lark tugged one of her own short curls, thinking for a long moment. In the kitchen half of the main room, Briar dropped a bucket on his foot and cursed loudly. "You may have drawn strength from your spell-thread when you contacted Daja," Lark finally said. "It *could* be that, since the thread contains magic from all four of you, made stronger by the spin. I *wish* we had time to work with it and see what it really is. I wish we had time to examine where you children are now. I have a feeling you've all grown in power—which is interesting."

Sandry gazed out the window, fiddling with the end of one honey-brown braid. "Does this mean I can work the same magic with you today? We could turn out more bandages."

"Just fruit, I think, and bread, and honey," they heard Rosethorn say. "It's too hot for porridge."

"I'll say!" Briar agreed.

"Come into the workroom," Lark said, getting to her feet. "We'll set you up on a bandage-width loom for this morning. This afternoon, well, we'll see."

"I'm to learn *real* weaving?" Sandry asked, skipping as she followed Lark out.

Glancing back at her, Lark smiled. "At long last," she replied.

Rosethorn put out tableware as Briar carried the fresh jars of milk, cream, and goat's milk in from the front step, where they had been placed by the Hub's kitchen staff. "I want you drinking milk today," she ordered.

"I only like it on porridge," he replied. "Elsewise, it's catlap."

"Then pretend you're a cat," she retorted. "It's good for you."

Briar stowed the jars in the cold box. "You ever been hit by pirates?" he asked. "Not here, I guess, since they never get in, but before?"

Rosethorn began to cut up bread. "My people are what Daja calls mud-rollers, over in north Anderran," she said, naming the country just west of Emelan. "Too far inland for pirates. Our village was attacked by raiders, once." She looked away, full lips tight. "Curse them. They raped my best friend, and left her like trash, because her face was scarred. They came for me, but my papa and brothers fought them off."

Briar growled. "To do *you* like they did your friend?"

Rosethorn smiled bitterly. "No. I was too valuable. They wanted me to do green magic for them, instead of Papa. They lost five of their own before they understood how determined he was to hang onto me."

"He musta loved you," suggested Briar, handing the butter to her. The word "love"—it felt strange on his tongue.

"He did. He also loved the profit I made for the farm," Rosethorn said, placing the bread on the table. "He was the richest farmer in our district, because of me. I didn't see milk go into your cup."

She never misses anything, no matter how I distract her, Briar thought gloomily, fetching the milk.

Tris came downstairs carefully, the covered nest in her hands. Its occupant was shrieking hungrily. "Is he sick?" she asked Rosethorn, holding out the nest with hands that shook. "Did I hurt him, is that why he's crying?"

Rosethorn took the nest. "He's hungry. Put some fresh goat's milk on to heat." Placing the straw-lined cup on the table, she lifted the handkerchief.

Briar, his fingers in his ears, stared at the bird. The young starling sat up very straight, beak wide open, shrilling at the top of his lungs. "Who'd've thought such a little animal would make so much noise?"

Little Bear, in what sounded like agreement, threw back his head and began to howl.

Sandry was just finishing breakfast, having eaten late after her first real weaving lesson, and Briar and Tris were cleaning the kitchen area, when horses clattered to a stop before the cottage gate. Ragged voices called for Lark and Rosethorn. The children ran after them, to see what was going on.

The squad of the Duke's Guard that had gone to the harbor looked much the worse for wear. All of them were scratched, sweaty, and dirt-streaked, with tiny holes and tears in the maroon shirts and breeches that had been spotless that morning. Two dismounted to struggle with a limp body tied over a horse. A guard held the reins of that mount as well as another with a much bigger form draped over its saddle.

"Mila save us, what happened?" Lark demanded, rushing forward to look at Daja.

Rosethorn glared at the sergeant. "I want an explanation and I want it *now*."

Briar shifted on his bare feet. The ground quivered. He felt roots—tree roots, crop roots, bush roots—straining in the ground. Rosethorn was upset. The plants wanted to go to her. Their eagerness to do it made the dirt tremble.

"They're all right," the sergeant told her tiredly. "But they did a big magic out in the harbor, the two of them, and now they can't even sit a horse. Had to bring them like killed deer. The girl was asleep when we landed—I don't think she even knows how we brought her home."

A guard draped one of Daja's limp arms around Lark's neck. Sandry went forward and took Daja's other side.

"She's a trooper, this un," the guard told them. "Acted her part good as a grown woman. Take care of her."

Sandry beamed at him. "We will."

As they bore Daja inside, Lark called over her shoulder, "Briar, get these soldiers a bucket of water."

He raced to obey, now that Rosethorn was calmer and the ground still.

Rosethorn went to the other lump. "Frostpine, too?"

The sergeant nodded, wiping her forehead with a weary arm. "We would've taken him home first. He insisted we come here and leave the girl with you, even if it was the longer ride from the harbor."

"You may as well leave him, too. He doesn't sleep in the Fire dormitory—he just has a dismal loft over his forge," Rosethorn informed them. "We can look after him as well as Daja. Bring him inside." Looking back, she saw that Tris was still there. "Tell Lark. We'll put Frostpine in my bed for now."

Tris obeyed. Lark had just finished putting Daja in her own room, on the ground floor, instead of trying to take her upstairs. She nodded when Tris said what Rosethorn had planned and opened the door to the other woman's room. Tris peered inside, curious. There were plants by the rear window—the only other window looked into Rosethorn's own shop and was shrouded by open shelves laden with clay dishes. There was a small altar in the corner, a clothes chest, a desk, and a bed. It was all plainer even than Tris's room. Does Rosethorn care about anything but plants? she wondered.

But she knew that was wrong. Rosethorn cared about Briar, and Lark, and birds. Maybe she was even beginning to care about Sandry, Daja, and Tris herself. If she thought about it, Rosethorn hadn't *really* barked at any of them—not painfully, as she had when the children had first come to Discipline—since the earthquake.

"You see?" Lark murmured. "No bloody hooks in the ceiling—not even a skull anywhere."

Tris blushed. She *had* been wondering something like that.

"In here," Lark called, waving to the guards who half dragged the unconscious Frostpine between them. Tris stepped out of the way.

As the guards passed her with their burden, the girl's sensitive nose picked up a funny odor: smoky and bitter at once. It was a familiar scent, but where did she smell it before? It was a heavy reek that clung to Frostpine's and the soldiers' clothes alike.

Curious, Tris went to Lark's room to see Daja. Sandry wrestled with one of the Trader's shoes. Tris helped with the other, sniffing the air as she did. Daja, too, was covered with that smoky odor.

"Look," Sandry whispered, once Daja's shoes and stockings were off. She touched Daja's right cheek. In the same place where the three at Discipline sported red weals, Daja had a nasty-looking scratch. "This has to be cleaned."

"Right here." Briar came in with a bowl of sharp-scented water and dry linen cloths. "Rosethorn says water with fresh yarrow crushed in will clean that ouch she's—*we've*—got." Pulling up a stool, he sat next to Daja, and dipped a cloth in the bowl. Wringing it out, he dabbed at Daja's scratch, gently cleaning it. "I'm glad you left that staff of yours upstairs," he told the sleeping girl. "I'd hate to have you bonk me on the head for cleaning this out."

Pain flared on Tris's cheek. Her own welt stung almost as much as when she'd first gotten it.

"Wish I'd been there," Briar murmured, to himself as much as to the girls. "All those ships . . ."

"*Shalandiru*," whispered Daja, eyes closed. "Oared warships, lateen rigs."

"I don't know if she's babbling or dreaming," remarked the boy. Reaching inside his sleeveless shirt, he brought out a little stone jar and opened it. "You'll *love* this," he told Daja. "My first batch of comfrey salve. It'll fix you up in no time, without even a wicked scar."

Sandry, whose uncle was a pirate-chaser, leaned over her friend. "What kind of *shalandiru?*" she asked, watching Briar gently smooth ointment on Daja's cut. Interesting, she thought. The weal on her own cheek was hurting less. "How many, Daja?"

"Front rank, ten dromons," Daja murmured. "Every other one alternating with single-bank galleys." She sighed.

"Front rank? There were more?" Sandry asked.

"It's a fleet, *saati*," whispered Daja. "I didn't get a good look at the second rank, or third—but they have them. I'm so tired."

"What's a dromon?" Tris wanted to know.

"Two banks of oars," Briar and Sandry replied at the same time.

"Most galleys just have the one," Sandry continued. "Dromons are bigger."

"And they have the thunder-weapon." Daja opened

her eyes and tried to sit up. None of them helped her. At last she surrendered. "Frostpine?"

"Rosethorn's room." Briar jerked his head in the proper direction. "He's as melted as you."

"What thunder-weapon?" Sandry asked Daja, frowning. "Was it that boom-thing we heard?"

"It sank one of the duke's galleys." A tear rolled slowly down one of Daja's cheeks, leaving a clean track in the grime. "It tore the sailors to pieces and blew a hole in the keel. We saved a few, but our boat was nearly full to start. Oti Bookkeeper give them credit, and send them to a kinder berth."

"A catapult stone would hole a ship," Briar pointed out. "You don't need thunder for that."

"A—a stone"—Daja yawned, her eyes sliding shut—"doesn't rip people and planks to shreds and fire the hold."

Tris started at this description of it. Leaning forward, she wrapped a hand around Daja's wrist. "Wait. This smoke, that's all over you and Frostpine." She ran a finger down the other girl's arm. It came away sooty. "This black stuff. The smell—it's not just wood smoke. Is *that* your thunder-weapon? It makes this stink?"

Daja nodded and slept again.

"Briar! Tris! I need you!" Rosethorn called, her voice sharp. "*Now*, not tomorrow!"

Briar placed his salve on the desk, along with the

water and cloths, and headed for the door. Turning back, he saw that Sandry was stroking Daja's hand, looking thoughtful. Tris was sniffing her finger. She had gone a strange shade of pale under skin reddened from yesterday's time in the sun. "That isn't Lark who wants us," the boy prodded. "Let's go, before she gets testy."

8

Ten minutes later, Briar and Tris walked onto the spiral road, both carrying empty baskets and message-slates: Briar's for Gorse, Tris's for Moonstream. Rosethorn had ordered special foods for Daja and Frostpine, while both she and Lark felt that the Dedicate Superior ought to know what now lay before Summersea Harbor.

"Dedicate Moonstream?" Briar asked a passing dedicate in Fire red.

"South gate," she replied and hurried on.

People and carts streamed by them on the road as they walked. These were local farmers, come to shelter inside Winding Circle's thick, high walls. In a way, Briar was glad to see them—it was like being back in the city of Hajra, though much cleaner. Little Bear and Tris did not agree. The dog was simply miserable. He had begun life as a stray in Summersea and had bad memories of crowds. Tris took each brush, each bump, each wait as a personal insult, her face getting redder and redder. Briar noticed that the wind had picked up, blowing every which way. He said nothing—the breeze helped ease the day's growing heat—but he kept an eye on his housemate. If she got *too* out-of-temper, he supposed he would have to make her relax, somehow.

Near south gate, the crowds evaporated. None of the refugees seemed to want to get too close to the cove and whatever lay in it. The woodshops and forges between the Water and Fire temples, however, worked at full capacity. To the left, in the yard around the school for physical training run by the Fire Temple, red-robed dedicates and white-robed novices drilled with swords, wide-bladed spears, and shields. Many of the boys that Briar knew from his short stay in their dormitory were holding their own weapons practice. There were a few girls among the boys; more girls and women wore red or white, and drilled as warriors.

Other red-garbed dedicates, in metal-studded leather jerkins and helmets, lounged around the south gate, weapons close at hand. The gate was closed and barred with huge timbers. In the deep tunnel that ran from it through the wall, both Tris and Briar saw the blaze of magic. Power shone from the many round stones embedded in the mortar that lined the tunnel walls.

"Here—you lot, scat!" yelled an armored dedicate. She wore the sleeves of her crimson habit tied up, baring arms as muscled as those of any blacksmith. For all Briar knew, she *was* a smith, like so many Fire dedicates. "This is no place for you!"

Triumphantly Briar held up the pass-token that Lark had given him before he and Tris left Discipline. Unlike the iron one, this was made of precious glass, with Lark's and Rosethorn's marks pressed into the sides. Lark had also tied a red silk cord so that it formed a cross on both sides of the round. That would get them anywhere in Temple grounds, she had told them.

The dedicate took it, looked it over, then spat on the ground. "The dog stays here," she ordered. "The baskets, too. Keep out from under people's feet on the wall. If you're ordered off, I'd better not hear that you argued. Who're you looking for?"

"Moonstream." Briar tried not to sound smug. "The slate in this basket is for her."

"Then you only need to carry the slate, not the whole basket." The dedicate returned the token but kept her hand out. The two passed over their baskets and ordered Little Bear to sit. To their surprise, he

121

obeyed, thumping his tail in the dirt. "She's right over the gate," the woman told them. "Behave yourselves." She bent down to give the dog's rump a scratch.

Reaching the steps, Tris growled, lifted her skirts, and began to climb.

"Now what's the matter?" demanded Briar, following her.

"I've been climbing a lot of stairs lately," she snapped breathlessly. "I'm starting to hate it."

"Maybe they'd go easier if you didn't climb like you hated them," he remarked. "Those flap-rags of yours don't help, either."

"Those what?" she gasped.

"Flap-rags. Skirts, and underskirts. Swap them for breeches, like Daja."

Tris halted. Turning, she glared at him. *"Breeches?* Like some—some street rat, or busker, or—or a Trader? I come from a decent family, I'll have you know, and decent females wear *skirts! And* petticoats!" With a final glare, she whirled and finished the climb to the top.

"Once a merchant, always a merchant," Briar muttered. The world was truly a marvelous place when a girl as smart as Tris Chandler clung to the very clothes that made her hot and cranky.

Moonstream and Niko were talking to a lean, red-headed dedicate in crimson. The two friends only glanced at the people they had come to find. Before them, visible at last, a pirate fleet lay in the cove. Like the fleet that Daja had described, galleys with two banks of oars alternated with single-bank galleys in the row closest to the land. Other ships lay behind them. Briar tried to do a rapid count, without success. The ships' images doubled and tripled and wavered before him, all lit by the silver glint of magic.

"No children allowed," a rough, high voice informed them. Strong, thin hands gripped Briar and Tris by the shoulder. They looked up. It was a long way to look: the redheaded man who'd been talking to Moonstream and Niko was over six feet tall. His short-cropped red hair stood at all angles, as if he often ran impatient fingers through it. His skin was weathered, his nose a thin, sharp blade. Tucked behind a neatly trimmed red beard, his mouth tossed out words as barks. His eyes were his only attractive feature, a deep shade of blue that drew the attention of anyone near him, whether they wanted to be drawn or not. His habit sported the black border of an initiate, or temple mage. The embroidered gold circle on his robe over the heart meant he was the First Dedicate—the head—of the Fire Temple.

"Things might get rough here," he told them now. "The guards shouldn't have let you up."

Briar held up the glass token and the slate. "We have this for Moonstream," he said firmly. "It's important. Honest."

"And I came for Niko," Tris said. Somehow she tore herself away from the Fire dedicate's gaze and out of his hold, to walk over to her teacher.

"She's with me," Briar said half-apologetically to the man.

"I guessed that. And I know who you are: Briar Moss. The gardening mage-boy. I've heard about you and your housemates. Been setting the Circle by the ears." He steered Briar toward Moonstream. "That's the weather-witch, Trisana Chandler. She knew we had a problem last night, correct? Nice bit of spotting. Smart girl, is she?"

"She does all right, for a skirt," Briar said, with a hooked smile.

By then they had reached Moonstream. "I notice you said that while Tris is talking to Niko and can't hear," she remarked, taking the slate. "By the way, this is First Dedicate Skyfire."

Briar shook hands with the lanky redhead, awed in spite of himself. They shared a homeland, Sotat. Five years before, Skyfire had been a legend as a general. On the death of his wife, he had given up his lands and armies and taken his vows to the gods of Fire. As First Dedicate of that temple, he was in charge of Winding Circle's defense.

"I'm glad Lark and Rosethorn sent me this information on what's in the harbor," Moonstream said at last. She handed the slate to Skyfire. "I know the duke will pass it on, but the sooner we get it the better, for some things."

Briar noticed that pinched lines had appeared around Moonstream's plum-colored lips. What harm could come to them, with Skyfire running the game? the boy wonderd.

"Niko, I'm telling you, it was the exact same smell," Tris repeated anxiously. "I don't make mistakes about smells. It's the same as the one on Bit Island."

"I believe you, my dear." Niko looked worn and anxious. "What it means . . ." He gazed at the sea, combing his mustache with his fingertips.

Tris waited a moment, but not more. Her curiosity was killing her. "How many ships are here?" she asked. "This is a different group from what's in front of the harbor, right? How many?"

"I can't tell," he replied. Seeing her frown, he added, "Like you, I can see they hide their numbers with illusions. But they're craven, these pirates. They hide behind layers of spells, done by at least a dozen mages. I don't yet have the key to all those spells, so I'm as baffled as you. No fewer than six dromons, I'm afraid, and ten plain galleys."

"The duke's navy will drive them off, won't they?" she asked, shading her eyes as she squinted out to sea. Something was taking place on two or three of the big galleys—*dromons*, two banks of oars, she told herself, fixing the word in her memory. Illusion spells rippled over them like heat waves, making it impossible to see anything but the closest ships clearly.

"The navy is scattered all along the coast," Niko quietly told her. "The few ships left in Summersea harbor are trapped now. We have to wait for the ships that are at sea to gather and come to our rescue. What *are* they doing out there?"

"Catapults." Neither of them realized that Skyfire had come over; both jumped at the sound of his harsh voice. "I can't see 'em—don't have to. The movements are right. It's what I'd be doing, right about now. Shurri knows they've got our range."

"C-c-catapults?" squeaked Tris.

"Could be worse," Skyfire told her, shielding his eyes. "They could be landing in the cove—which is what they *will* do, when they learn the spell-net down there is gone."

Tris remembered what Daja had said about the spell-net and flinched. Winding Circle had no army, just the dedicates of the Fire Temple, those who wanted to help them, and mages. Would they be enough? Would pirates take this place and burn her only home? Would they take her and—

"Sometimes a good imagination is a bad thing." Niko put an arm around her shoulders. "The defenses around the rest of Winding Circle are in perfect condition, and *we* aren't exactly helpless here."

"Certainly not," commented Skyfire, with a bark of

a laugh. Raising his voice he called, "Six mages—Air and Fire, if you please."

The top of the wall was dotted with red- and white-robed soldiers, mingled with dedicates from all four temples. Now Tris saw that all of the non-warriors had the black-bordered robes of initiates. Three in yellow, initiates from the Air Temple, and three in red came over to Skyfire. He paired up Fire and Air, then pointed out their stations along the wall, about fifty yards apart, all facing the cove. "By air," he told them, still watching the shimmering vessels. "By air—a hundred feet up, no less. I want a solid shield—no sloppiness. No cracks. Get ready."

Tris eyed the pair closest to her. They were rapidly threading copper wire through the wide links of a two-foot-long gold chain. Once that was done, the initiate in yellow hung dull gray stones on small hooks in the wire, spacing them well apart. The initiate in red did the same thing with stones that looked like amber, flint, and onyx.

"Copper is an air element," Niko mumured in her ear. "The gray stones are pumice, a stone of air. Gold—?"

"Fire, and protection," said Tris.

"Very good. And onyx, amber, and flint are protective." Niko kept his voice soft, in order not to distract the initiates. "Everything in the device has been repeatedly spelled for protection against trouble from the air. Daja would call it a *bijili*, a thing that stores magic. With such a tool, these mages don't have to use much of their own power—which they might need later—to protect this section of the wall. All they need do is call on the strength of the metal, and the stones—"

"And the temple walls," added Skyfire. Tris jumped. She hadn't even thought he was listening. "Like everything else here, the walls themselves hold magic, put into them over—here we go."

Two black, round balls soared into the air between the ships and the walls. Squinting at them, Tris shivered. She got the impression of magical signs and of her eyes being thrust away from the balls. Quarreling breezes yanked at her hair until her kerchief fell off, and her unruly curls went flying. She scrambled for the cloth.

"Why bespell catapult stones?" she heard Niko ask.

"Too high!" someone down the wall, an archer, yelled, shielding his eyes to follow the missile's flight. "They're too light for stones, Skyfire!"

"He's right," growled the dedicate. "What in Shurri's name—?"

Higher and higher the dark balls rose.

"They'll be over your shields!" cried Skyfire. "Raise them, raise them—"

Tris shook, terrified. It was as plain as day that the things would pass over the wall higher than a hundred feet. She would be ripped to pieces, like the dead of the Bit Island tower and the men Daja had seen on that galley!

Winds swirled over the wall, coming from everywhere. They raced around Tris, knocking Skyfire, Niko, and Briar out of the way. Tris barely noticed; her eyes were on the round balls as they began to drop. She reached blindly for the winds.

They shrieked, spinning tighter and tighter, shaping themselves into a funnel. The narrow end of the funnel swirled around her hands, tearing at the skin. The wide end stretched and stretched as the whole thing grew.

Tris clenched her fists, then opened them.

The funnel jumped free of her, racing into the sky to scoop up the twin balls. Turning, it paused, as though trying to decide which way to go.

A giant, invisible hand pressed those on the wall. A breath later, a dull crack boomed through the air. The funnel blew apart. In another breath, a dusting of soot, dirt, and splinters rained down on them all.

Tris sneezed. Niko drew a clean handkerchief from his overrobe, wiped her cheeks with it, then gave it to her so she could blow her nose.

"I must rethink my opinion of weather-witches," Moonstream said, her voice clear and calm in the ringing silence on the wall. "It seems they do more than just bring rain."

Skyfire leaned down so he could look straight into

Tris's eyes. Nervous, the girl backed up a step, then two, until she collided with Briar. The boy held onto her. Two more steps, and they would both go off the wall.

"Girl, can you do that cold?" Skyfire wanted to know, making his voice as gentle as he could. "Or do you have to be scared? If it comes to that—" He grinned, showing far too many teeth for Tris's comfort. "I'm sure I can think of ways to scare you when they launch those things. The other way *is* much friendlier, of course."

"Those weren't catapult stones," remarked the Air mage closest to them. "Stones aren't that light."

The Fire initiate with him added, "I don't know if we can put a shield so high—"

"Lower it, then!" cried Briar, pointing to the ships. "Here come some more!"

"Don't let those things strike the wall!" barked Skyfire.

By then the snap of the catapults' release had reached the defenders' ears. All three sets of mages, seeing these balls were aimed at the wall, called on their magic again. Their metal and stone devices began to glow. Both Tris and Briar could see washes of silvery light rising ten feet higher than their heads as well as dropping out of sight, to cover the stone beneath them.

"The wall won't hold?" Tris asked in a tiny voice. She was trembling all over, vibrating in Briar's grip.

"We don't know," whispered Niko.

The air slammed around their heads, causing nose-bleeds. The mages lurched, but kept their feet without letting go of the metal they used to guide their power. Dirt and rock sprayed into the air. Most stayed on the other side of the barrier, but enough came over it to give everyone and everything a thorough dusting.

"They blew two holes in the ground," a blue-robed dedicate called when there was quiet again. "Big ones."

"You children, off the wall, *now*," ordered Skyfire. "Tris, think about what I said to you. The rest of you, spot-shields only—block each of them as they come in!"

"Go on," Niko told them. "I'll see you in a while."

"Come on," Briar whispered in Tris's ear. He got an arm around her waist to steady her. Tris's shakes were much worse. "Another one of those and you'll faint for certain."

Nodding weakly, she let him help her down the stairs.

"We still have to get that food for Daja and Frostpine and your bird," he remarked.

"I know," Tris said. "I haven't forgotten."

"And I'm a bit gnaw-ish, myself," he added. The further she got from the top of the wall, the stronger she seemed to be. Still, he hung onto her until they were on the ground.

"You're *always* gnaw-ish," she retorted, sitting on the bottommost step.

Little Bear raced over to them, wagging his tail and yapping. The guard who had kept him and their baskets followed, taking a water bottle from her belt. "Exciting up there, is it?" she inquired. Uncorking her bottle, she wiped the mouth on her wrist and offered it to Tris.

The girl took it with a muttered thank you and gulped thirstily. "Too exciting for me," she said, offering the bottle to its owner. The dedicate motioned for her to pass it to Briar instead, and Tris obeyed.

"What's going on up there?" asked another warrior, a novice. "All that banging made my curls go straight." Since he was shaved bald, even Tris could tell this was a joke.

"The pirates have got some odd new weapon," Briar told them. He shook the bottle and looked at its owner. "If you don't mind waiting, I'll refill this for you at the Hub."

"No need," the woman said, taking it from him. "We've our own pump at the guardhouse. New weapon, is it?" She spat on the ground. "Had to be something, to get those dogs thinking they could try us again." To Little Bear she added, "No offense to four-legged dogs."

"You aren't scared?" Tris asked, wiping her face again with Niko's handkerchief. She could see dirt and rocks all around them; some of the blasts had

132

been felt down here. The gate-tunnel would have amplified the noise, too.

Their guardian shrugged. "New toys or no, they'll have to step pretty to dazzle old Skyfire."

Briar nodded. "He was never caught napping that *I* heard of. Come on, Coppercurls," he urged Tris. "It's almost midday. Bet Gorse has a chicken or some pasties with my name on 'em." He gathered up the baskets and whistled to Little Bear.

"Don't fret, youngster," the novice advised Tris when she rose, shakily, to follow. "They'll need a much bigger cracker to open up *this* nut."

Some of the other guards laughed, including the woman who had so much confidence in Dedicate Skyfire. Others, Tris noticed, looked as uneasy as she felt.

You'd think differently if I hadn't stopped those first two bang-things from dropping in here, she thought, trotting to catch up to Briar. And you may end up thinking differently anyway, if more get past the mages on the wall.

They entered the Hub kitchens through the outside doors, not those that opened onto the central stair. Even before they went in, they were startled by the amount of noise that poured out of the building. Little Bear sat, refusing to go into such a madhouse. Plugging an ear with her free hand, Tris took a basket from Briar and followed him inside.

They were engulfed by steam and heat. Shurri's

Forge, deep in the earth, couldn't be any hotter, Tris thought. "Is it always like this?" she yelled.

Briar jumped out of the way of a novice staggering under a full tray of bread loaves. As he passed, the novice suggested that Briar's mother had done something very unlikely with a snail.

"And your dam with a wharf rat!" shouted Briar cheerfully. To Tris he said, "No, never!"

Someone grabbed his shoulders. "Thieving little urchins *outside*," ordered a dedicate in flour-streaked blue. "And if—"

Briar grabbed one of his hands, bending the dedicate's smallest finger back on itself. He grinned savagely, white teeth flashing against his golden skin, as he exerted pressure. The dedicate howled.

Threading her basket until it rode higher on her arm, Tris grabbed the boy's hands. "You won't fix anything if you break his finger!" she yelled in Briar's ear. "You—"

Suddenly the three of them came apart. Flying backward, they landed outside on their behinds: Tris, Briar, and the dedicate. Little Bear yelped madly. The man scrambled to his feet, to come face-to-face with a big-bellied dedicate who stood in the open doorway. The newcomer scowled at all of them impartially. He was two inches short of six feet, with the black hair, brown skin, and the almond-shaped eyes of a far easterner. His hair was gathered into a tail and clubbed to lay forward on top of his head, after the custom of the men of Yanjing. He had a broad face, with a long, flared nose, a wide mouth, and a thick, trimmed beard. It was impossible to tell what color his habit was, under the stains and scorches. Tris thought it might be red, then wondered if it was blue, green, or yellow. She had never been able to decide which temple this man belonged to. Perhaps, since kitchens combined all the elements, the dedicate in charge of Winding Circle's belonged to all four temples.

"Dedicate Gorse!" cried the Water dedicate. "I was *trying* to eject a thief—"

"If you *must* grab things, Dedicate Withe, you may grab thirty chickens and kill them for me." Gorse's voice was deep and booming. He spoke very precisely, with a thick accent. "Make sure to bleed them in the proper manner. *Now*, please. No more grabbing my visitors." To Briar and Tris he said, "Too many mouths to feed today. We are very busy."

"That boy is a known thief!" cried Withe, pointing at Briar. "He was skulking in there—"

Little Bear growled. Tris seized his collar.

"Briar Moss never stole from me." This time there was a dangerous note in Gorse's voice and a hard glint in his black eyes. "Chickens, Dedicate Withe. And think as you kill them about the fate of those who accuse without proof."

The man stomped away, red with humiliation. Briar held out the slate Rosethorn had given them.

To him Gorse said, "No more breaking the fingers of kitchen help. I need their hands. Break a toe, if you must." Taking the slate, Gorse looked at Tris. "How is your bird? Briar said you have a baby bird to raise."

She smiled wryly. "He's loud."

"That's good," said Gorse, nodding with approval. "Healthy lungs are loud ones. I will grind fresh meat for him, so he builds his strength. Cooked eggs we also have plenty of, for the soldiers. And what is this?" He read the note on the slate, frowning. "Pork liver or beef liver? Three kinds of beans? We have peas and seafood stew. This is rich food she wants—very heavy, very strong."

"It's to build up Frostpine and Daja," Briar explained. "They worked magic in the harbor, and now they're so tired they can't sit up. Rosethorn says they need all that."

"Then we give Rosethorn what she wants, or *she* will come to get under my feet. You two wait in the shade, by the stair. Too many people like Withe are under my feet today." He picked up the baskets the children had dropped, his big hands dwarfing the thick, strong handles. "I will fill these. Wait." He leaned inside, and reached for something. One at a time, he handed a pair of heavy buns to Briar with his free hand. "One is for Trisana," he told the boy with a meaningful look and vanished into the kitchen.

"You never said he was nice," Tris accused as they

136

walked to the entrance that would let them into the Hub.

"You should've figured it out your own self," replied Briar, his mouth full.

"I never really talked to him before." Tris sank down on a bench near the central stair, the dog at her feet. A lone runner seated against the wall nodded to them, then dozed off.

Tris ate her bun by picking off a piece at a time and chewing carefully. Strange, she thought as she began to relax. The racket from the kitchens didn't reach this part of the tower—and yet only the walls and a set of double doors lay between the two.

Magic, no doubt. Was everything here magic?

One of the kitchen doors eased open, releasing a burst of sound and a slender male figure in breeches and overrobe. He closed the door and turned into the light.

"Tris! Briar!" Aymery was clearly startled, and not entirely happy, to see them. He fiddled with his earring, then smiled so warmly that Tris wondered why she'd thought he was unpleasantly surprised to find them here. "Now this is a happy coincidence."

"Depends on who it's happy for," Briar remarked. "I can't believe Gorse let you escape without giving you something to eat."

"Gorse?"

"The dedicate in charge," Briar said, frowning. "Everyone who goes in there meets Gorse."

"Maybe on other days," said Aymery. "Right now, I think he's busy. What are you two doing here?"

Briar explained their errand, but kept his other thoughts to himself. He'd crept in at night, in the days after his arrival, when a full belly was still cause for excitement, and he'd filled it as often as he could. He'd hidden under tables and kept to the shadows when all the fires were banked. He'd come as meals were being prepared and people rushed in and out, carrying food to the wagons for those who didn't eat in the main dining halls. Before dawn, at high noon, at midnight—it didn't matter. He was never in those kitchens for longer than a minute or two before Gorse showed up and gave him something to eat. He thought that Gorse might sleep in the Hub, but that was not the point. He'd seen Gorse do it with anyone who wasn't kitchen staff. He supposed it was *possible* that Gorse had not seen Aymery today, with refugees pouring into the temple community, needing to be cheered up with a good meal.

It was *possible*. It simply wasn't likely.

The doors popped open. Out came Gorse himself, their baskets in his hands, and a smaller, covered basket threaded onto one brawny forearm. Tris took charge of one of the large baskets and the little one; Briar took the other.

"Have we met?" Gorse inquired, looking at Aymery.

"Aymery Glassfire," the younger man said, with a

half-bow. "I'm recently arrived, come to pursue studies at the library."

"A mage," Gorse said. "I know how it is. If you are hungry, reading late, come here. Someone is always on hand."

Someone meaning *you*, thought Briar, but he kept it to himself.

To Briar and Tris Gorse said, "Do not linger. Go home quickly and store what is not to be eaten *right away* in your coldbox. The little basket is just cookies, for afternoon." With a nod, he disappeared back into his kingdom.

"If you don't mind, I'll come with you," Aymery said, walking outside with them. "I'm hoping your Lark and Rosethorn will take pity on me. They want to move a Trader caravan leader and his wives into my rooms in the guesthouse. If I don't find something quieter, I'll end up with a piece of floor in the boys' dormitory. No one can study under those conditions." Reaching out, he gripped the heavier of Tris's two baskets. "Let me help you with that."

Tris scowled and yanked it away. "I've carried worse than this," she growled as the three of them followed a path that cut across the wide loops of the spiral road. "I used to carry *two* baskets this size to market, when I was at Cousin Uraelle's, *and* back."

"*Back?*" Aymery's eyes widened with shock. "Up that ghastly hill? But you were just a little girl—"

"I earned my keep," Tris said with pride, hoisting

the larger basket to keep it from brushing a flower border.

"But she had *servants*, the old miser—"

"A woman came three days of seven, for big chores," replied Tris. "But she had to be watched. She was lazy. Cousin Uraelle was bedridden, so I had to keep an eye on things."

"The old skinflint," muttered Aymery. He took the other large basket from Briar, which suited the boy just fine. "She was rich enough to afford servants. Did she leave you anything when she died, at least?"

Tris shook her head. "Not a copper."

"Then where did the money go? She must have left it to *someone*."

"House Chandler. They have to have a ship named for her on the seas forevermore."

Merchants, Briar thought. I'd've left it for something useful, like a garden in a place like Deadman's District, or the Mire. He grinned, amused by the idea that he would ever be in a position to leave money to anyone when he died.

They were just crossing the crowded road between the loomhouses and Discipline when three loud, sharp cracks split the air to the south. A horse reared, screaming in fright: Aymery dragged Briar out from in front of it. Oxen drawing a handful of carts lowed, the white showing all the way around their eyes. Little Bear plumped his behind on the cobbles and yowled; dogs and babies among the refugees did the same thing.

"Thanks," Briar said to Aymery, when the man let go. "Little Bear, stop it, or I'll tell Rosethorn on you." The pup fell silent.

Tris stared at Briar, sweating. "You think it was more of those booming things?"

"I'm sure of it," the boy said, opening the gate to Discipline. "Come on. Let's get inside."

Rosethorn, Lark, and Sandry were all at the big table, working. Tris went immediately to her bird in Rosethorn's workshop. She could hear his shrill voice. Uncovering the nest, she saw the starling was awake and alert. Seeing her, he opened his beak wide.

"In a moment," she said, and covered him up again. She helped Briar to stow the baskets' contents in the coldbox, eager to find the ground meat and egg yolks that Gorse had put in. The nestling squalled. "In a moment" was not what he wanted.

"If we didn't already have Frostpine and Daja in our own rooms—well, Rosethorn and I will be sleeping in our workshops as it is," said Lark, when Aymery made his request.

"I feel guilty, not having anyone when they're laying pallets down in all the dormitories," Rosethorn admitted.

"I don't mind a pallet, here or in the attic," Aymery told them.

"You don't need one." Sandry looked up from her weaving. In the time since Briar and Tris had left, she had managed to put nearly a foot and a half of cloth on the narrow loom that Lark was teaching her to use. If pressed to comment, she would have said it looked no worse, though not much better, than the weaving she had done the day before. "If Daja says it's all right, I'll sleep in her room, and Tris's cousin can sleep in mine." Getting up, she went to see if Daja was awake enough to ask.

She was, and gave her permission immediately. With that settled, Aymery went to get his things from the guesthouse.

"Now," Lark told Tris and Briar as Rosethorn heated fish stew, and Tris prepared meat and egg balls for her nestling. "What did Moonstream say when you found her?"

The nestling was fed, and the stew hot, when five sharp crack-booms shattered the noontime heat one after another. Outside, people cried out. One woman screamed, "What is it?" over and over, until someone hushed her up.

Tris was shaking. Lark and Rosethorn, looking grave, took the stew to their invalids.

"No one's ever seen anything like this?" Sandry whispered to the other two children.

"Not that we heard," Briar muttered.

The five of them were just finishing their own midday—not the stew, which was needed to build up Daja's and Frostpine's strength, but cold beef, cheese, and vegetables from the garden—when a runner stumbled in the door.

"Moonstream asks for the senior mages to be on the wall by south gate when the clock strikes one," he gasped, and ran out again.

"That means us," Lark said, rubbing her face tiredly. "I don't know how much good I'll be for this." She rose with a sigh and looked out the window at the clock. "We have a few minutes to get there, at least."

"I know what Moonstream wants." Frostpine stood in Rosethorn's doorway, his dark face ashy with exhaustion, as he leaned on the frame. "If they're using those—those boom-stones, or whatever they are, down at the cove—"

Lark helped him over to a seat.

"Thanks, my dear," Frostpine said. He leaned forward, supporting his weight on the table. "All those bangs are coming from south gate." Everyone looked at him, not sure what he was getting at. "I heard you say we have pirates in the cove. They'll be trying to land—and that piece of the spell-net is ruined. The southern approach has no protection but our handful of soldiers and the war-mages—who are only human. How long can they hold off pirates and their mages? And how long can they keep the pirates from landing those catapults on the shore, where they can bombard all Winding Circle?"

"Before we didn't need anything but the spell-net," Rosethorn commented. "No one could fight it—"

"Because once invaders touch the net, they have no idea of where they are, or what they do," said Frostpine. "The net is still protecting the rest of the wall on the west, north, and east. But the cove . . . I think Moonstream needs you senior mages who can walk to find ways to defend the south gate, and the beach."

Rosethorn slowly grinned, showing her teeth. "I can be of use, then." She strode into her workshop, crooking a finger at Briar. "Come on—you'll help me." The boy obeyed.

Lark drummed her fingers on the table, thinking. Abruptly she commented, "Sandry, continue with this kind of weaving while I'm gone."

"But Lark—" protested the girl.

Lark raised a hand to quiet her. "I know we'd thought to go back to magical weaving this afternoon, but I can't risk you trying it alone."

"I'll be careful."

Lark smoothed a lock of hair away from Sandry's

face. "Some of the spells we've done with you four—the weaving spell, the spell Niko used with Tris to see what happened at Bit, the one Frostpine and Daja used on the harbor chain—those are called great-spells. Without a senior mage who understands great-spells to guide them, young mages have been known to get so caught up in one that they die. They feed their magic and their lives into the pattern of the spell, without ever realizing what they were doing."

"My best friend died that way, twenty years ago," Frostpine commented, resting his head on his folded arms. "He was building a lead pattern—it was to be a window in the shape of a thousand-petaled flower, one that would hold and give off sunlight on the gloomiest days. He wanted to impress our master, and he burned up right in front of my eyes."

Sandry gulped and nodded. "I'll stick to this, I promise," she said, patting the small loom. This weaving lacked the feeling of power she'd had the day before, as she watched the novices stagger away with baskets full of new bandages. On the other hand, she was enjoying life too much to risk losing it so foolishly.

Rosethorn and Briar returned. Briar carried a cloth bag, Rosethorn a bottle and a cup just big enough to hold an egg. To the eyes of all three children present, the bottle gleamed white with magic. Placing the cup next to Frostpine, Rosethorn poured it half full of green liquid. "Drink," she ordered. "You and Daja must be able to move, just in case."

Frostpine made a face. Lifting the cup, he dumped its contents down his throat. "*Auugghh!*" he yelled, his voice stronger than it had been since his return from the harbor. "Are you trying to *kill* me, woman?"

"If I mean to kill someone, I do it," Rosethorn told him. "I don't *try.*" She poured a lesser amount of green liquid into the cup. "Give this to Daja, and put the bottle back in my workshop. And keep resting, while you can." To Lark and Briar she said, "Let's go."

Frostpine whistled the dog back when Little Bear would have followed the three of them. The ashy tone was fading from the man's dark skin, and his back was straighter. Getting to his feet, he took the cup in to Daja.

"I hope they'll be all right," Sandry whispered to Tris.

"Maybe bring our cord out here, just in case," the other girl said quietly.

Sandry nodded, and went to get the circle of lumpy thread.

When they reached the top of the south gate, Briar decided it had been a bad idea to invite all the senior mages up. The racket was worse than in a houseful of geese, he thought, and the noise made about as much sense. There was Crane, First Dedicate of the Air

Temple and Rosethorn's main rival, waving thin arms as he argued with Niko and Moonstream. Gorse was nowhere in sight. Surely anyone who could blow people out of the kitchens without touching them was a senior mage, but perhaps his cookery spared him from follies like this. He also didn't see Skyfire near the Dedicate Superior. That was because Skyfire was in position further down the wall, beside a pair of mages, scowling at the invading fleet.

Lark waded into the crowd. She put a hand on one yelling dedicate-initiate's shoulder, spoke in another's ear. Both looked shamefaced, tucked their hands into their habit sleeves, and stood back to let her through. Touching, smiling, talking quietly, Lark worked her way through the noisy gathering, leaving calm in her wake.

"There's more to Lark than meets the eye, isn't there?" Briar asked Rosethorn.

"We'll make an initiate of you yet, boy, if your perception keeps improving," Rosethorn said. "Come on. If we get arguing with this lot, we'll lose time." She headed for Skyfire with Briar in tow.

He looked out to sea. The illusion-spells were off the fleet: He guessed there were ten dromons in all, and fifteen plain galleys. Inching between the ships were long boats laden with men, small catapults, and weapons: a landing-force. In the prow of each boat stood a man or woman—mages, Briar guessed, to protect the raiders from Winding Circle's magic. Not just

148

from magic, either, he realized, seeing that all along the southern stretch of the wall, dedicates and novices readied catapults of their own. Beside each stood an open barrel filled with globes: animal skins that held a dreadful-smelling liquid.

"Battlefire?" he asked one of the mages near Skyfire, pointing. The woman looked and nodded.

Briar shivered. Once in Hajra, three ships, survivors of a pirate attack, had limped into harbor when he and some friends were playing on the docks. Each had been hit by the jelly called battlefire. One ship burned as it came and sank inside the harbor's mouth. The other two had docked to off-load their dead and wounded. The sight and smell of scorched flesh had given Briar nightmares for months.

Rosethorn waited until Skyfire was done speaking with a runner, then told him, "You're so busy planning how to weave magics, shielding that and blending this, that you forget it doesn't *have* to be magic alone."

Skyfire glared down at the stocky woman, thin nose twitching. "Only shields will protect us from those catapults and the boom-stones," he snapped.

"And the cove?" she asked. With a wave she indicated the stretch of open dirt below them. It was pocked with deep craters and reeked of boom-stone smoke.

"That's why we have archers, not to mention *these* clackers up here," Skyfire snapped, glaring at the crowd around Moonstream. "They just haven't been used yet."

Rosethorn poked Briar so he would show the red-headed dedicate the bag he carried. "Brambles," she told Skyfire, naming the seeds that she'd ordered Briar to put into it. "Rosevines. Sea buckthorn. Briars." She grinned at the boy. "Sea holly. Milk thistle, Namorn thistle—and a few things here and there to help it all along."

Briar tried not to smile. Before he'd tied each fist-ful of seed into a square of cloth, Rosethorn had drenched them in a liquid that did for plants what her other tonic did for weak birds and worn-out mages.

Skyfire lifted one of the small bundles in his hand. "You think you can grow enough of a barrier to hold off that landing force?" he asked, skeptical.

"Get that seed all over the ground, and Briar and I will see what we can do," she told him firmly. "All your warriors need do is launch the bundles—Lark will make sure they open to scatter the seed."

Skyfire rubbed his chestnut beard, then took the bundle from Briar and waved to a handful of soldiers loitering nearby. One of them was the woman who had taken charge of Little Bear that morning; she winked at Briar and stood at attention for Skyfire's or-ders. "Get two of these little balls to each of the cata-pults along this quarter of the wall," he said. "Load them immediately. Get them into the air. Cover all the area not shielded by the spell-nets."

"Get Lark," Rosethorn whispered to Briar.

Lark was coming already. "I'll do more good over here," she grumbled to Rosethorn quietly. "Why is it no one wants to work with anyone else?"

"*I* don't want to work with those idiots," said Rosethorn. One of the war-mages standing close enough to hear snorted.

They heard a snap. The catapult nearest to them hurled small gray bundles high in the air. From one sleeve Lark brought out a square of cloth, its edges unsewn and fraying. Her eyes on the cloth bundles as they soared over the ground, she tugged two edges of the bit of cloth, yanking out threads three and four at a time. The bundles came apart, releasing clouds of seed into the air.

Rosethorn made room for herself and Briar by a notch, so they could lean on the raised stone beside it. Briar was pressed against it, with Rosethorn close behind him. He breathed in her funny scent: pine, dark soil, hints of basil and aloe. With her at his back, he felt almost as if he rested in the arms of Mila of the Grain herself, though he quickly assured the goddess there was no blasphemy meant.

"Are you ready?" inquired Rosethorn.

His eyes were on the seeds as they drifted to the ground. "I think so."

"The magic is a pattern of reaching into the ground and growing with the seeds from there. I'll pass it through you, so you can follow it, and me," she told him. "Just don't think you can do this with growing things all the time."

"They need to grow slow," he replied. "So they're strong clean through."

"That's right. I'm glad you understand. All right, breathe in—"

Closing his eyes, Briar drew breath in through his nose. The two of them sank down through the cold, white-flashing inside of the wall—

What is all that light? Rosethorn demanded within his mind.

With a half-blink's time of thought, he explained about Tris's magicked spectacles and the glitter of magic that the four now saw. Then he and Rosethorn broke through the wall, and the earth outside the wall, and the spells that held the ground under Winding Circle together. They were in soft dirt now, spreading themselves wide through the slope down to the water.

The seeds were on the surface. Rosethorn called to them, breaking into hundreds of magical threads, each seeking, then entering, a seed. In her magic was the power of stone-cracking vines, of pine seedlings that could grow over a farm in a handful of years, mixed with the demand for haste that only humans felt. Briar saw how she made her magic a root system. All that was left for the seeds to do was to stretch out branches and limbs, instead of fragile shoots. Once he knew what he saw, he reached with his magic, running it through the pattern she had placed inside him. Connecting to hundreds of seeds to her left, he fed them a rush of strength. Bushes and brambles leaped into growth, exploding from the ground, throwing out leaves and flowers as if a spring were compressed into minutes.

Rising above the ground for a look, he discovered his third of the barren slope was covered with the fresh, pale color of new growth. Rosethorn had two-thirds of the open ground; her plants were dark green, the thistles already a foot high. Her vines and brambles fought to cover as much surface as they could, reminding Briar of a litter of puppies scrambling after a meat-covered bone.

Nearby he could hear a series of dull cracks. Something thudded, shaking his spine.

Fire erupted in his shoulder and on his back—not the back of the body still up on the wall, but on his magic's back. Briar yelled, looking around. Five more craters had been gouged out of the earth. They smoked and glowed like dying embers, filling the air with the stink of burning leaves.

He could feel Rosethorn trembling behind his true body. "Concentrate!" she snapped when she realized he was thinking of her.

Briar urged his plants forward through the magical root-pattern. He coursed along their veins, filling them with anger. Bramble wove itself into thistle clumps and braided with rosevines. Sea holly mingled with sea buckthorn to form solid walls of stickers. Moving out into the plants' skins, he gave particular attention to each and every spine and thorn, urging them to grow, and to grow sharp.

To give them fuel, he fed them his hate for pirates on shore leave who thought it fun to kick a street boy or to break his arm as a warning to pickpockets. The plants would wrap and cling like the muck of the sewers that he'd once lived in. Emotion ran through his garden like sullen blood, a dose of misery, resentment, and fury that they would be eager to pass on.

More cracks: overhead, boom-stones bounced off glowing circles in the air. The circles turned and shifted as the mages used them like shields to keep boom-stones off Winding Circle. Once a ball was knocked from its path, it either blew up—or fell.

Roars shredded the air as four boom-stones exploded high overhead. Near the base of the wall two fountains of dirt and rock erupted, spraying everyone above. Rosethorn and Briar screamed in pain and rage as their greenery was torn to oozing pieces.

"Look at the shore. Can you speed it up?" Skyfire asked, his voice booming in their bodies' ears. Sending their power aboveground, Rosethorn and Briar looked at the water's edge. The longboats had reached the shore. Three-foot-high plants awaited them where Rosethorn had been working; Briar's were a little more than two feet tall. It wasn't enough to stop them, not for long.

154

"Deeper," Rosethorn growled. "I'm going deeper into the spell."

"How?" Briar asked her. "Show me."

"No. Keep working as you have. You aren't ready for this."

Somehow she moved him, until his pattern fed into the plants she had brought along already. Part of her remained there, while the rest wove itself into Briar's old area. She flexed around him, then pulsed, expanding like a bursting sun. Where he had gone only as deep as each plant's skin, keeping most of his attention for their weapons, Rosethorn *became* each and every root and stem. She collapsed the growth of months, even years, into a breath. Everything grew.

It was a comfort to find that her thorns, needles, and stickers weren't as long or sharp as his. She didn't hate enough, he decided. She had never been tossed through the air by pirates celebrating a big haul or dropped because they were too drunk to see where she was thrown. Briar shared that with her plants as their leaves and stems lengthened. Their spines stretched for him, looking for a pirate to sink into.

Something louder than the earlier boom-stones whooshed through the air, near enough that his real body flinched. There was a dull thud and a sudden wash of heat. Briar threw up an arm to shield himself—to shield his plants—from the fire. Rosethorn screamed, and screamed again.

The raiders had landed. Setting up catapults, they

155

had launched skins of battlefire into the green tangle before them. On landing, the skins burst, spraying jelly everywhere. Their mages had only to touch the stuff with flame to make it burn. Sheets of fire sprouted between the raiders and the wall.

Nearby, someone was screaming. Further down the wall, a gout of battlefire had splashed through the mages' protections. A warrior-dedicate stumbled burning through a notch and fell into the brambles. Other dedicates were beating out flames with their habits. Two novices dragged a charred body out of the way. It looked like the woman warrior from that morning.

Rosethorn sagged against Briar. He dragged her arms around him, taking her weight on his shoulders. She was groaning deep in her throat. Suddenly he was terrified. *Sandry! Tris! Da—*

We're here. Power flooded in, making every hair on his body stand up. Clutching the thread circle, the girls were twined together like a spun cord, Sandry a gold-white strand, Daja red-orange, darker—weaker— than the other two for today, Tris a brilliant blue shot through with white. *What do we do?* they asked.

Rosethorn refused to let go of her magic and her ties to the plants. She clung to them, despite the pain from all the burning. Everything continued to grow frantically.

Like this, Briar told his friends. He slammed into his pattern, taking them along. They roared through its crossings and turnings, bringing it to life in the mind they now shared. Now they saw, as he did, how to build the magical fire until every green thing in the cove had to grow fast or explode. They fed the thorns and stickers with their anger and bitterness. Daja had her own memories of pirates, as did Sandry. Tris was furious at these parasites who burned and killed and made her new home unsafe. The four boiled through every root, branch, vein and needle, forcing them higher, longer, thicker, sharper—definitely much, much sharper.

They knocked Rosethorn out of the pattern without knowing it. Ablaze with anger and fear, they were unable to feel the hands that shook and tugged at them.

"Trisana, you aren't listening to me!" a cracked, sharp, familiar voice said in her mind. She smelled vinegar and mildew. *"You beggar me with your extravagance! I'm just a poor widow, with barely enough to live on, and you eating me out of—"*

Tris's hold on their joining faltered. "Cousin Uraelle?" she whispered. "You're dead."

"No more beef at this table, not at these prices! Copper penny for turnips? You didn't bargain enough! You—"

The others felt Tris shrink and fade as that voice railed on and on. She was losing confidence. She was losing her grip on the pattern.

A fiery spindle appeared in the children's mind, whirling counterclockwise, unraveling things. Their bond with the plants was coming unspun. Briar's grip on the magic relaxed. Sandry, recognizing Lark's work, dropped away. In Discipline, Frostpine held Daja's fingers, wrapped tightly around the lumpy thread, and gently pried them open, one at a time. *Oh, all right*, she thought, and let go of the magic herself.

Someone pinched Briar's earlobe hard. "Don't *ever* break loose from me like that again," Rosethorn said, her voice ragged. "You could have killed yourself *and* the girls."

"But they were *hurting* you," he protested.

Lark, shaking her head, tucked her spindle away. "You should have warned him," she murmured.

"You're not helping," snapped Rosethorn. To Briar she said, "A little pain is bearable, to protect this place. And at least we've done *that*." She pointed to the ground outside the wall.

He could see nothing but stems, vines, and very long thorns. In some places the growth was nearly six feet high; nowhere was it shorter than four feet. It reached up to, even a little way into, the water. Search though he could, he found no sign of the longboats, their catapults, or the pirates who had manned them.

"They escaped?" he asked, his knees starting to wobble. "They got away?"

Skyfire uttered a barking laugh. "Never had a chance. They're somewhere under all that. They're never coming out, if that's what worries you." The Dedicate Superior had joined them. To her Skyfire said, "Can we bring up the *entire* spell-net for the night? Not just the east and west segments?"

Moonstream shook her head. "Hardbottle village—half of their people haven't made it in. We told them we'd keep the north gate open until dawn for the stragglers. As far as anyone knows, the pirates haven't gotten around the spell-net in the east. If we had a way to make them stay put once it gets dark, that would help."

Skyfire looked at the silent cluster of senior mages. Briar realized they must have drawn close to watch him and Rosethorn. "I want a fog around this place so thick I wouldn't know my mother if I stepped on her foot," Skyfire ordered. "Those villagers will have the road, and our guards, to guide them in, but anyone in open country had better not dare move, for fear of breaking their necks. And if some of *you* can't drum it up, maybe I'll just get all four of these young people up here. We'll see what *they* can do."

"Unnecessary." The voice—stiff, haughty, male—belonged to Dedicate Crane. He looked down his very long nose at Briar. "I submit that senior mages are superior in their control. Your children need to work on theirs," he told Rosethorn, his rival.

Briar just grinned tiredly and gave Crane a careless salute.

Half an hour later, Tris still had not forgiven Aymery for putting Uraelle so vividly in her mind. "I can't believe you did that to me," she said for the dozenth time, wrapping trembling hands around the cup of tea that Frostpine had made for the girls. The two men had been going through some books Aymery had brought up from the guesthouse when the girls received Briar's call. Somehow Frostpine had guessed what the children were up to and insisted on trying to break the link. Aymery had made the first important dent in their union with Uraelle's voice—Tris knew that as well as her cousin did. "You couldn't have used someone else?"

"She was the best one I thought of," he replied with a shrug. "And Asaia Bird-Winged knows I heard her yattering on enough when I was small." Seeing Tris's puzzled look, he explained, "We lived with her for two years when I was your age."

She winced. "I'm sorry. You *still* didn't have to—"

Niko stalked in the door in a swirl of robes and steel-colored hair. "What is the *matter* with you four?" he cried, black eyes flashing.

Daja, Sandry, and Tris drew closer together. Frostpine, brewing a fresh pot of tea, looked at Niko with raised eyebrows. Aymery pretended to inspect the nestling's box.

"Have you no hold on yourselves?" Niko continued furiously. "Can't you tell when you're about to pass your own limits? You could be *dead* at this very—"

"They were hurting Briar and Rosethorn." Sandry forced herself to meet Niko's blazing eyes. "We thought they were *killing* Rosethorn."

"*She* is a senior mage who knows the difference between momentary discomfort and true danger, which none of *you* seem to understand! Have you not learned that you simply cannot throw yourselves into the great magics as if they were bathtubs?"

"We're *just kids*," snapped Tris, lips trembling as she fought tears. "We haven't had time to learn hardly *anything!*"

"We've learned some," Daja added quietly. "But not huge things."

"At least they *did* help," growled Briar. He had followed Niko from the gate, determined to get home under his own power. And he had managed it—just. When Sandry helped him to the table, he couldn't bring himself to object. Once seated, he glared at Niko. "They didn't stand there like a bag of bleaters, waiting for mamma's leave to romp."

"Those *bleaters*, as you call them, are mages who know better than to enter a pattern-magic without the primary mage's permission." With a sigh, Niko sat on the bench next to Tris. "They wouldn't have been able to." Looking at each of the girls, he said wistfully, *"You* shouldn't have been able to."

"That was *pattern-magic* they interrupted?" Aymery

wanted to know, eyes wide. "These—children broke into—"

"If it's something 'children' can't do then we kids didn't do it." Briar glared at Aymery.

"Drink this." Frostpine pressed a mug into the boy's hands. "It'll make you feel more human."

Niko rested a hand on Tris's shoulder. She yanked away and turned her back to him, still fighting tears. She had been scolded so rarely at Discipline that it hurt twice as much as it had before, when it had happened so often.

"I'm sorry I lost my temper," Niko murmured. "You frightened me. I didn't know if you would be alive when I got here."

Tris shook her head, refusing to look at him.

"I think the bird wants supper," Frostpine said.

It was true; the nestling was screaming. "You're not supposed to yell or be loud around him," Tris said to no one in particular. "It upsets him." Picking up the nest, she carried it into Rosethorn's workshop.

"I'll help." Sandry collected milk and honey from the coldbox and followed Tris.

Frostpine stared at the door to Rosethorn's bedroom, rubbing his bald spot. "Will she stay with Moonstream or at the Water Temple tonight? I don't think she ought to sleep on a pallet in her shop— she'll be drained—but she won't let *me* sleep in there. I *could* go back to my forge."

"She's coming here," replied Niko. "Some of

Skyfire's people are carrying her up. Lark's with them. It's just taking them more time than it did me."

Briar slumped forward against the table, resting his head on his arms. "She hates being carried, even when she can't walk," he mumbled. "Sleep in my room, Frostpine. She won't mind if *I'm* in her shop. Just let me neaten up." Getting to his feet, he stumbled into his room.

Frostpine raised his arms over his head with a groan. "I'll make Rosethorn's bed." He went into her room. Aymery started to brew more tea with the water Frostpine had set to boil.

Niko said nothing for a while. When he spoke, it was to Daja. "I thought you were depleted—exhausted—from this morning."

The black girl shrugged. "I had Rosethorn's green stuff to drink," she replied. "Same as Frostpine. It did a lot of good."

"But the basic dose of tonic can restore only so much. Where did you find the strength to help Briar so—dramatically?"

Daja shrugged again, looking at the table.

"I must know, for your own sake. Did you drink more tonic than you were supposed to?"

Daja shook her head. "It's the string we spun in the earthquake," she told Niko. "It made Sandry feel better this morning, and it made me feel stronger when she had me touch my lump."

"A lump?" Aymery inquired, then winced. "Sorry, Master Niko. Must I leave?"

"No, that's all right," said Niko, holding up a hand to silence him. "Your lump?" he asked Daja.

"There's a lump in the thread circle for each of us. I touched mine, and I felt better. Not as strong as the rest, when Briar called for help, but lots better than when I got up."

When Sandry returned, Niko said, "I wish to see this string of yours."

She put her hands on her hips, glaring at him. "Tris is crying. She's never been under catapult attack before. She's frightened."

"So are we all," Niko said. "I will go to her, but in a moment. The string, Lady Sandrilene." He held out one long, thin hand.

Her little nostrils flared, as if she scented trouble. "It's *ours*."

"It could have gotten you into trouble that all of your teachers combined could not have saved you from. I will have it, if you please."

His black eyes met her blue ones and held them. Watching, Daja and Aymery held their breaths.

It was Sandry who looked away. She fished the circle of thread from a small pouch that hung around her neck, inside her dress. She hesitated, then gave it to Niko.

The moment he touched it, he jerked, dropping it on the floor. "Gods above!" he whispered.

"What is it?" Aymery inquired. "A magical artifact?"

"It's a *bijili*, isn't it?" Daja wanted to know.

Aymery looked at her.

"The *mimanders* use them. They keep things in *bijili*—winds, or strength for when the *jishen* come and they're worn out, or even just for light. A *bijili* can be a crystal, or a glass bubble—" She stooped, and picked up the circlet of thread. "Or knots in a string."

Niko opened his handkerchief on the table and pointed to it. Daja reluctantly put the circle onto the linen square. He folded up the cloth and put it into his shirt pocket. "Until the four of you learn control, I'd rather see you play with coals from the fire than something like this, even if you did create it yourselves."

"How about we play with boom-stones?" asked Briar, leaning against his door frame. "I wouldn't mind getting a look at one of those—before it went boom, anyway. Long before."

"As would most of us," Niko said grimly. "I've been watching them all afternoon, and can't for the life of me tell what's inside their containers. They're even better spelled against magic than battlefire. If we knew how they were made, we—"

"Why can't you put me down?" demanded a cross voice outside. "People will think I'm dying if they see me carried in by two hulking lads—"

Briar smiled dreamily. "She's home."

165

Lark entered first, looking as tired as everyone else. Then two armored warriors, a dedicate and a novice, eased through the door sideways. They had made a chair of their arms and were carrying Rosethorn between them. She was soot-streaked, her hair black with sweat. Despite the irritated vigor in her voice, she had so little strength that she couldn't sit up, only lean again the novice.

It was Kirel; he looked positively harassed. "We brought her," he told Niko. "And believe me, it wasn't easy."

·10·

Exhaustion rolled in with the fog that Skyfire had ordered. Once he'd made his peace with Iris, Niko tried to meditate with the children, to work on their grip on their emotions while working magic, but gave up after first Briar, then Daja, then he himself nodded off. Supper came up from the Hub, but no one wanted the trouble of setting the table or of cleanup later. Those with the strength nibbled on bread, cheese, fresh garden vegetables, and smoked fish from the coldbox; everyone but Aymery seemed half-asleep.

No one wanted to go to the Earth Temple baths

after supper, either, but in the end the need to get clean was stronger than weariness. The children, Aymery, Lark, Frostpine, and Niko managed the trip to the baths.

Briar made certain that he was bathed and out well before the men; the girls and Lark, he knew from past experience, would take a while to finish. Bone-weary as he felt, he still managed a weak trot back to Discipline, Little Bear at his heels.

Rosethorn was sound asleep when he crept by her open door. He doubted that she would waken for some time yet, which was all to the good. If she caught him going through Aymery's belongings, she would make his life a misery.

That he had to do so, he was sure of. He liked Tris's cousin, but in Deadman's District he had liked a great many people who he couldn't trust as far as he could throw them. Aymery made him feel untrusting. He tried to tell himself he wasn't jealous of the way Tris looked at her family-approved mage cousin, the one who'd been kind to her, but living with Rosethorn tended to strip the illusions from a boy. Briar *was* jealous, a bit, but he told himself that had little to do with it. Something about Aymery was not right.

Before they'd left, the boy had prepared a bowl of the uneaten chicken stew, carefully going through it for any bones. Now he put the bowl on the floor for Little Bear. As fast an eater as the pup was, it would still take him a while to devour so much. Eating, he would care about nothing else, such as where Briar was, until he was done.

Before he got to work in Sandry's room, Briar made sure that its front window was open. The rest of Discipline's residents would come in the back. If he left the room through the front window and walked around to reenter the cottage through Rosethorn's workshop, no one should guess where he'd actually been.

Aymery hadn't brought as much as Briar had expected: a small chest with plenty of brass fittings and a large, impressive-looking lock; a larger chest that stood open in the middle of the floor; two saddle-bags. The larger chest was a third full of books; the rest was clothing. He could find no hidden compartments. A look into the saddlebags revealed necessaries like shaving gear, money, jewelry, a traveling writing desk, a few more books. Now, here was Tris's cousin, liking to dress well—too well for a student, thought Briar, who had seen many young scholars when they came to Deadman's District for rough fun—who'd mentioned a stay of some weeks the night before. He didn't have enough pretty clothes for that. If he were a poor student, as most were, then he'd have a reason for a small wardrobe—a small, *cheap* wardrobe. But he wasn't poor, was he? If he were, then why did he buy a shaving mirror of the finest Hataran glass, and silver-backed brushes and combs? If he were poor, how did he pay for the small pouch of earrings, and a collection of gods-amulets in precious metals? The trunk with his books and his saddlebags were all serviceable enough and had seen plenty of wear. They looked like normal student gear. He might well have brought those to the university from Capchen.

But the smaller trunk . . . The smaller trunk was new, and it had cost Aymery something.

Here were contradictions, then. Being poor was the only excuse for a small wardrobe for several weeks' stay—but everything about the goods he *did* have screamed of money. If he were a rich student, then he would have packed enough for a lengthy stay, and he hadn't. Aymery was lying about something, that was plain.

Briar knelt to examine the smaller chest. Merchants, he thought, shaking his head. Only a merchant would buy such an expensive-looking piece of trash. The pricey wood inlays were veneer, thin sheets of costly wood laid over cheap stuff. There were cracks in them already. He could pop the wide straps off with a chisel and his own hands; the nails that bolted them to the wood were no sturdier than the veneer. And the lock! The only reason to buy this item would be for so large and ominous-looking a lock. It was the kind of lock that screamed "safe"—and it was no safer than a bread box.

Briar appreciated a merchant's son's trust in craftsmen. It had made his life easier back in his thieving days. It would make it easier now.

Reaching into his waistband, he drew out the slim packet of lock picks he'd made since his arrival at Winding Circle. Normally he kept the packet under a loose board in his floor. Niko frowned on him so much as carrying a hide-out knife for protection— which he did anyway, because there were plenty of respectable uses for a knife. There were none for lock picks.

He chose two and delicately inserted them in the keyhole. Immediately he felt the burn of ordinary protection-spells running through his fingers. Softly he whispered the words of the standard canceling-spell that he'd had to learn by heart when he was four. The burning stopped. A nudge of one pick, a tickle of the other, and the lock opened as smoothly as butter.

"I love me," he whispered.

The box was divided into velvet-lined compartments under a velvet-covered top tray. He recognized items in the tray: a deck of fortune-telling cards in a silk bag, sticks of chalk for drawing magical circles, shallow bowls for things like herbs, water, oil, and salt, a handful of talismans for the working of spells. Here were ink-sticks in various colors, stone trays for mixing ink, drawing brushes, and reed pens. All of these things would be used for the working of magic; it was the basic kit. He lifted out the tray.

Light blazed, so bright that it nearly blinded him. Briar sat back on his heels, knowing that if he stuck a hand into that light, it would burn like acid. The funny thing was that he knew how to break this spell—the secret was expensive, but not at all hard to learn. Spells to foil common protection-magic could be bought and used by anyone, whether they had magic or not, which didn't exactly make him respect Aymery's judgment. True, he'd said he was specializing in illusion-magic, but what was Briar supposed to think of a man who couldn't be bothered to put his own spells on his treasures?

He never looked for any kind of search, a voice whispered in Briar's mind. He expected everyone to believe in what he claimed to be. He expected to deal only with his own kind, not with someone used to thieves and nasty folk who talk one way and do another.

Briar made the signs of the more costly charm and blew on the light. It vanished. In the compartments were some bottles, packets, and something square, in a velvet bag. Picking up one of the bottles, Briar sniffed and nearly sneezed. Cinnamon oil and poppy. The container was half-empty.

"Bad, Aymery," he murmured. "Very, very bad."

One vial contained a gray powder. He glanced at the label. While he could only read individual letters, and not even all of those, he wasn't stupid. Rosethorn had a bottle labeled with most of these same marks. She'd said it held a sleeping mixture. She had also taught him the meaning of a number of signs commonly put on labels. One of two on the bottle full of gray powder meant "extremely strong." He didn't know the other but memorized it. Perhaps one of the girls would know what it was.

The other bottles had no meaning for him at all. Opening the bag, he drew out the flat thing inside. It was a mirror, set in a glass frame shot with bubbles of gold. The mirror itself was black and glossy.

Inside it, shadowy forms moved. A voice in it said, "My dear sister, you worry too much. Things are nearly in place."

Briar dropped the mirror back into its container and thrust it into its compartment. Hurriedly he began to put everything back: he could hear Aymery and Niko approaching as they talked about some book or other.

Crawling out the window, he wondered, If all the scrying-mirrors in Winding Circle broke last night—why is Aymery's still whole?

It wasn't long before everyone went to bed. Niko stayed at Discipline, dozing off in a big chair padded with blankets and cushions. Even Little Bear was sound asleep, on his back with his paws in the air, in front of the cottage altar. He hadn't so much as stirred when everyone came in from the baths.

Tris was the last child to go to bed, saying good night to Aymery—the only one still awake—after her nestling got his last meal of the day. She had put bed off, partly because she disliked the thought of that steep climb to the attic. Partly it had been listening to Aymery talk of his university studies; to her relief, he hadn't mentioned going to see her father after that first conversation. Partly it was the thick fog that now pressed against the cottage, muffling even the noise made by new refugees coming down the road from north gate. Tris hated to be inside during fog. She wanted to be out, walking in the middle of a cloud that had managed to come to her.

And if they throw more boom-stones despite the fog? she wondered as she hauled herself over the last step and onto the attic floor. A fine thing, to be out in the open and have one of those things drop on you!

She looked up at the planks that hid the thatch over their heads. How well *might* the roof hold up, if struck by one of those things? Certainly not as well as the deck of the galley that had been struck by one that morning.

Shurri Fire-Sword, defend us, she thought, hurrying to her room. Trader and Bookkeeper, Trickster, I don't care who, keep those things off us!

"You took long enough," Briar said from the shadows by her window.

For a moment she was so terrified that she thought she would faint. Groping one-handed, she found her empty washbasin nearby and threw it at him.

He ducked. The basin clanged to the floor.

"Tris?" Lark called tiredly from downstairs.

"Sorry!" she yelled.

Briar picked up the basin, examining it. "Now you have a dent."

"I ought to dent *you*," she hissed.

"You tried." White teeth flashed in the gloom. "You missed."

Tris gently placed her nestling, who hadn't so much as peeped when she threw the basin, on her desk. Finding her steel and flint, she lit a candle with hands that shook. "How did you sneak in here?" she demanded, still keeping her voice down.

He yawned and pointed out the window. Tris understood. She had left this room sometimes by dropping onto pillows that were conveniently placed on the roof of Rosethorn's workshop, then jumping to the ground. If an ungainly thing like her could do that, someone like Briar could easily climb up. "Aren't you too tired for this?"

"What I had to tell you can't wait."

"*I* say it can. Get out."

"Listen, Coppercurls—your cousin's as wrong as they come. And don't throw anything else; the grown-ups need their rest."

For a moment her throat worked, but no sound came out. Air gusted around the room, making her wall hanging flap. She wrapped her fingers around the nest to hold it still and finally squeaked, "How *dare* you! How—"

175

His eyes met hers; the words dried to ash in her mouth. This was Briar. They had kept each other alive during the earthquake, and they'd watched clouds get born together. She'd only just started to teach him to read, but she could tell already that he would love it as much as she did. He had kept her from falling off a wall only that morning.

"Please say you're joking," she whispered, and sat heavily on the bed.

Now that she had calmed down, he sat beside her and told her what he'd found. "Where's he getting his money?" he asked when he was done. "You don't buy the things he's got on a student's allowance—"

"How would *you* know about student allowances?" she asked, trying to braid her unruly hair. The air was gusting again, plucking locks from her hands.

"I learned awful quick it's not worth the trouble to pick their pockets," he said. The hair on the back of his neck prickled. There was more going on in here than just the wind picking up. "They hardly ever have two coppers to rub together—if they have anything, they spend it on books." When she made no comment, he went on, "From what you say about your family, they won't pay extra money to anyone, even their future mage, till *after* he's shown what he's good for. So where's he getting his money? And maybe he *says* he came to study for weeks, but he didn't pack like it."

"He could have left his other things in storage at

the guesthouse." Tris spoke dully, trying to reject what he was saying. Her heart thudded. Her skin prickled, tingling. At that moment she hated Briar for telling her these things, for sounding so sure.

"I bet it was him that I saw on the Hub staircase, with the invisibility spell—but why was he there? I bet whatever blew up the stuff in the seeing-place, he put it there."

"You never saw a face. It could've been somebody else." Why hadn't he just gone straight to Niko, or to Rosethorn? The tickling along her skin got hotter. Now she could feel her pulse banging in the veins of her neck.

"Why sneak into the kitchens?" Briar wanted to know.

"Don't tell me Gorse would notice *everybody* in that madhouse today."

"But Gorse does. He—" Briar glanced at the window and froze.

A thin, three-fingered brand of lightning felt its way along the window ledge like a hand that searched for a place to grip. The scent of charred wood drifted on the air. They could see black streaks where the lightning touched the wood.

Briar seized Tris's arm. "Get hold of yourself!" he whispered.

Tris shook Briar off and went to stand before the window. It wasn't really lightning, exactly—just a thread of it. She stretched out a hand.

"Don't!" Briar hissed, too frightened to move. "Tris—"

The gold, skeleton arm reached for the girl. Briefly its three fingers touched hers. Tris felt the brush of white-hot light, as if something she had only seen could be felt. Her curly hair began to rise.

The lightning folded in on itself, rolling out the window.

Briar put his head on his hands. "If I had a mother, I'd want her right now," he muttered. "Can't you do *anything* small?"

Tris brushed the fingers the lightning had touched against one cheek. They were warm, nothing more. "Do I want to?" she asked dreamily. The lightning had been so *beautiful*. It didn't hurt her feelings. It didn't tell lies. It was above everything ugly. People didn't matter to it.

She wished that people didn't matter to *her*. "Aymery isn't what you think."

"Neither are you," he muttered. "Look—I think we're safe tonight—Little Bear will let us know if Aymery gets to bumping around, and Skyfire is going to fog this place in. But come morning, we've got to tell. I think your wondrous cousin's working for the pirates." He padded out of the room.

Not Aymery, Tris thought, flinging herself back on the bed. Not him.

She'd been having daydreams of Aymery returning home, making the family a nice profit somehow, and then bringing her in to be his assistant, or apprentice, or something. In those imaginings, her family had seen that Aymery's judgment was right, that they had done Tris a wrong when they got rid of her. They would want to make amends. They would want her back.

She wished the lightning would return and touch her again.

Her eyes burned, but it was impossible to cry. She was too tired. The day had been long already. It was only seven in the evening: If the fog hadn't set in, there would still be light in the sky. It didn't matter. Putting her spectacles on the floor and covering her eyes with her arm, Tris slept.

The Hub clock was chiming midnight when she began to wake. By the time the bell that marked the half hour called through the misty air, she wasn't a bit sleepy. With a sigh, Tris sat up. Disgusted, she realized that she'd gone to sleep in her dress and stockings. Everything was hopelessly rumpled. About to undress, she heard a creak downstairs. If someone else was up, maybe they could talk. She wasn't about to go back to sleep. For one thing, she was hungry.

Gathering up her spectacles, she padded out into the attic and over to the opening where the stair pierced the floor. She walked softly, to keep from rousing the other sleepers in the house.

The person downstairs was being very quiet. He—

or she—was also in the dark; there was no sign of lamp or candle.

Another soft creak, and two more. Whoever made them was coming toward her. One last thump, and then nothing. The walker had gone outside, through the back door next to the stair.

As quickly as she dared, Tris climbed down the ladder and peered outside. A dark shape vanished into the dark fog, walking through Rosethorn's garden.

It's him, a disgusted magical voice said.

Tris jumped and whirled. Briar was behind her.

Then why didn't Little Bear bark? she demanded.

He hasn't so much as rolled over since I went to bed. Briar frowned. *We'll lose Aymery if we don't move. Or should I just wake Niko?*

Tris walked down the path, peering into the fog. *He's going for a stroll,* she insisted.

He always tippytoes when he's on a nice, happy stroll, agreed Briar with false cheer as he followed.

Tris glared at him. She heard someone stumble and curse, not far away. Aymery was as blind out here as she—or *was* she blind?

Stretching out her power, she pushed through the dark, wet curtains around them, as if she sent ripples through a pond. There he was, the one moving thing that picked through the clinging mist. Puckering her lips, she blew, thinking of dueling sea breezes. Little puffs of air battled in front of her, shooing the fog to one side of the path or the other for a few feet ahead. Now Tris was able to move forward at a trot, with a bit more ground visible, while the fog let her know Aymery's direction. Briar was right behind her.

We're going to ask him, and he'll explain, Tris said as they passed through the grape arbor. *You'll see.*

She clung to that idea, trailing her cousin around the baths and around the temple itself. There, in front of the temple porch, her foot caught. She sprawled face-first onto the ground. She had tripped over a curled-up novice who used her armor for a pillow. Briar hit the legs of a snoring red-robed dedicate, who was stretched out like a felled tree near the path. He stumbled and righted himself. Neither sleeper as much as moved.

Huddled shapes lay all around as far as the pair could see in the mist. Briar knelt and shook the sleeper who had tripped him. The man simply rolled over. They were alive, then, but sleeping as if drugged.

Now we know why Aymery was in the kitchens, Briar remarked. *And why Gorse didn't see him. Aymery made sure he couldn't be seen, so he could put sleeping potions in the food. A good thing we kept to the food we already had, right?*

When they looked up, the fog had closed in; Aymery was gone. They could barely see each other.

She was beginning to think Briar was right. She *hated* that. Her elbow and knee throbbed from her fall. Aymery had vanished and could even now be letting their enemies inside. . . . He could be doing *anything*, while she stood here blind!

Tris *slammed* the fog up and forward, as hard as she could. The air shuddered; mist exploded away from her chubby form. Trees bent and groaned, leaves flapping. Sleepers rolled away from her. Briar hung onto a temple pillar and sent his power into the ground, racing to protect the trees from the pain of ripped greenery.

Aymery, suddenly visible, was thrown into the wall beside the north gate.

Tris glanced up. The fog was racing into the night-dark sky, colliding with storm clouds that had been forming higher up. Had she started something? I can't think about that, she decided, and stomped up to her cousin. "Aymery!"

Briar ducked behind a tree. He'd let Tris do the talking. Let the maggot think they were alone, and he might speak truthfully.

Aymery lurched away from the wall. "What are you doing here?"

Despite the heavy snoring all around them, the cousins spoke quietly, as if they might wake someone. "Aymery, please—you aren't—" Tris swallowed hard. "It looks bad, Aymery. It really does."

"Don't worry," he said earnestly as she approached. "I'll protect you. Nothing will happen to you."

"What about my friends? What happens to them?" Tris stopped a foot away from her cousin.

"I'll do my best, and—you'll just have to trust me, that's all. In case you forgot, I *tried* to get you to leave, remember?"

"You lied even then, didn't you? About my father being ill?"

"I didn't want you here for this. But you were mule-headed, and I never got another chance to talk you around. Just stick close to me, and I'll speak for you to Enahar. He's their chief mage."

"Why are you working for them? They're thieves, and murderers—"

Aymery sighed. "I owe them money, Tris—more than you could imagine. It was gambling, and—and other things. Enahar gave me a loan, but there was a price. That's how the world is." Going to the gate, he wrapped his hands around one of the locking bars and started to lift.

Briar cursed. This was cutting things much too fine. *Daja! Sandry!* he cried. *We need help and we need it fast!*

Tris ignored the boy's call. "This is a *temple community*," she reminded Aymery. "What kind of loot do you expect to find?"

He stopped pushing on the heavy bar to stare at her. "Don't you know *anything?*" he asked. "There are spell-books here, centuries old, which teach things like making diamonds from coal and rubies from blood. Bespelled weapons, devices—they have a mirror that will let even a non-mage spy on anyone at all. And mages are the highest-priced slaves anywhere—there's all kinds of ways to keep a mage that won't hurt his ability to do magic."

"I see those ways work on *you*," she said flatly.

Aymery sighed. "Yes, they do. See this?" He tugged at his earring. "It was made with my blood and with Enahar's. It binds me to him. If he thinks I'm about to betray him, he can use it to kill me. And don't tell me to get rid of it. I can't, not so long as I'm alive." His smile was crooked. "I tried."

The winds rose as Tris swallowed hard. "Can't you turn it on him?"

Aymery shook his head. "I'll just bear with it—he'll free me when my debt's paid. This raid should do it, with plenty left over." One locking bar was up. One remained. Someone outside pounded on the gate.

Tris grabbed Aymery, yanking him back. The growing winds whipped her skirts. "You can't do it!"

Unsheathing his knife, Briar hurled it straight at Aymery. A puff of angry air knocked it away.

Tris whirled, her hair flaring out like a halo. "Stop it!" she yelled, furious.

Briar searched two snoring guards and found their knives. "He's not listening!" he shouted. "And that isn't the Fire Temple guard waiting outside, is it, Aymery?"

For answer the young mage punched Tris, knocking her back several feet. She hit the ground and lay there, stunned.

The gate exploded. Aymery went flying, landing not too far from Briar.

The boy didn't waste time thinking. The tree that had concealed him had low branches—he jumped for a limb, pulled himself onto it, then climbed until he was ten feet up. Looking at the gate, he saw that the smoke that filled the hole in it began to thin. Armed men and women rushed through the gap, holding kerchiefs over their noses and mouths. Their leader, a bandy-legged man in a breastplate and leather breeches, stopped to survey the scene before him. Briar looked frantically for Tris. She lay without moving a few yards from the pirate leader, her eyes closed.

Aymery sat up, groaning. His face was dappled with blood, and he had a nosebleed, but Briar thought he didn't seem badly hurt. The chief pirate walked over to him, sword in hand.

"Aymery Glassfire?" he demanded, stuffing his kerchief into a pocket.

"You didn't need the black powder," Aymery muttered. "I was—"

The pirate ran him through the chest, his rumpled face showing no feeling. "The boss says your deal's off," he told Aymery's body. Bracing himself with a foot on the dead youth's chest, he dragged his blade free.

Briar held very, very still. If the leader glanced up, he was dead.

Instead the little man looked at the people who followed him. "Start killing," he ordered. "We don't want 'em at our backs later."

Briar gulped and closed his eyes as first one sword bit, then another. He'd seen cold customers in his time, but to murder people in a drugged sleep—

Hail dropped like an avalanche, pummeling and bruising. Briar screamed with his own pain and that of every green thing under that hard fall. It ripped leaves to shreds, stripped twigs from branches, and left bruises on every inch he couldn't protect.

It stopped as suddenly as it began. Below, the pirates huddled on the ground, cloaked in white, like everything else he could see. Rising, they shed hailstones like diamonds. They staggered when they tried to move, dizzy from the pounding.

"Where did that *come* from?" demanded the leader. "Get some torches out o' the temple, *now!*"

The sleepers began to stir; the hail must have roused them. Tris lurched to her feet, coughing and retching, half bent over from Aymery's blow and her fall. The leader advanced on her, sword at the ready.

Silver flickered in the air, tracing a ropelike line that coiled around the pirate's neck. He jerked back, fighting for air. The temple warriors lurched to their feet and attacked the still-numb pirates. Briar climbed down as Daja and Sandry ran around the corner of the temple. Sandry flicked her magical rope, throwing the pirate into the air. She didn't wait to see where he came down. She and Daja came to help Tris instead, reaching her at the same time as Briar. The four clung to each other as fighting raged all around them. Taking deep breaths, they surrounded themselves with a wall of sheer power, made like a net with their interwoven magics.

"Warn someone—" croaked Tris, swaying. "Where's Aymery?"

"We told Lark and Niko," replied Sandry, hiding her face as a pirate killed a novice close by.

"Aymery?" Tris asked Briar.

He shook his head. If she hadn't seen, he didn't want to be the one to tell—

The air filled with a powerful glow that made even their magical barrier turn dim, leaving no shadows, no area where mischief would be worked unseen, no place to run. That was Niko. Frostpine and Lark revealed their presence when cloaks, necklaces, bracelets all came to life, twining around pirate arms and legs, tripping and wrapping, hobbling. Swords jumped into the air on their own, to come down hilt-first on pirate heads. Within seconds, the invaders were disarmed and surrendering, their hands in the air. The attack was over.

Lark, Frostpine, and Niko approached the barrier,

and the children let it down. "Are you all right?" Lark demanded. "What happened? How did you come here? Where—"

Tris looked around frantically. She'd seen her cousin knocked flying after he'd punched her, right before she'd blacked out.

Aymery lay near a giant tree that had lost all its leaves. Moaning, she went to him, streaming tiny lightnings as she ran, making the air hiss as she passed. Putting her ear by his open mouth, trying to hear him breathe, she rested a hand in the middle of a huge soggy patch just under his breastbone. It came away almost black in the over-brilliant light that Niko had made, black and rippling with tiny sparks. Speechless with horror, she stared at her cousin's face. He stared back, dark eyes wide and unblinking, looking not so much terrified as surprised.

Tris began to rock, small bits of lightning jumping from her to him. She wanted him to wake up. She wanted him to stop scaring her. "How *dare* you hit me!" she cried, and pummeled him.

No one wanted to touch her. Even Niko was reluctant to venture near the fiery darts that played around Tris. Sandry was just as afraid as anyone else: Tris was scary now. She was also in pain. Afraid or not, Sandry couldn't let that continue. Making herself take first one step, then another, she approached her friend. Steeling herself to actually put a hand on Tris's shoulder was a little harder, but she did it.

The lightnings played around her hand, tickling her skin. Her hair struggled to rise out of its braids.

Tris looked up at Sandry, her eyes red and puffy. Then she took a deep breath and held it. Releasing it, she breathed in again. The lightnings faded, then vanished. With a sigh of relief, Sandry put both arms around her friend.

"It was for *money*," Tris muttered into Sandry's nightgown. "He said they enslaved him, but he didn't seem to mind. He was going to let people die for . . . for gold."

Daja and Briar heard this as they came over. "That's what *jishen* do," said Daja grimly.

Sandry and Briar tugged Tris to her feet and turned her away from Aymery's body. "Let's go home," Sandry whispered.

"I think it's for the best," Niko said quietly. "There's a lot of sorting-out to be done here." He had come over to talk to them by himself. Lark was helping wounded dedicates to the temple steps; Frostpine and a dedicate in red were rounding up all of the prisoners. "I'll speak with you later—Moonstream and Skyfire, too, in all likelihood. For now, you should go. We need to get this gate repaired," he said loudly, walking toward the dedicate working with Frostpine.

Daja tugged on Tris's arm. "Leave him," she said, meaning Aymery. "He would have made slaves of us all."

Tris shook her off gently. Kneeling, she unclasped

the earring from her cousin's flesh. Then she let her friends lead her home.

Even there, she had little peace for the next two hours. The four had to explain matters to their teachers and to the dedicate who had been in charge of the north gate guard. From the dedicate-guard they learned that the spell-net that protected the temple walls had been left inactive on the north road, so nearly fifty villagers could reach Winding Circle. Now the guards suspected that the villagers were dead or enslaved by the pirates, who had come ashore and made their way around Winding Circle's protections to seize just this chance.

The story was told again, after a groggy Moonstream and Skyfire examined Aymery's belongings. By then, Tris had heard Briar tell of Aymery's death. The mist that she had blown out of the northern part of Winding Circle had returned. When she heard the clock tower's fog-muffled bells strike two in the morning, she retreated to her room to sleep.

11

The starling woke Tris, squalling for breakfast. The people in Discipline were still asleep as she staggered down to warm milk and honey for her bird. Little Bear, hardly able to walk in a straight line after his drugged supper, had to be let outside. Tris waited until he came back, then closed the door against the fog that still clung to everything.

An hour later, Tris lurched downstairs again to feed the nestling meat-and-egg-paste balls and water. She began to think she would have done better to drown him. Any worries she had about making him ill through ignorance had evaporated. No dying creature possessed such lungs.

When he woke her for a third time, she gave up. She cleaned her teeth and dressed, then went to heat his goat's milk and honey. There were signs that someone else had been up, made tea, drunk it, and gone. Sticking her head into Lark's workroom, she saw that both Lark and Niko were missing—the chair-bed and the pallet on the floor were empty.

Stopping now and then to feel Aymery's earring, tucked into a skirt pocket, Tris drew water from the well and set it to boil. She washed the juice and tea cups left by their after-midnight visitors, started the porridge, put more tea-water on, and dusted the main room. She lost herself in small chores, keeping grief at bay as well as she could.

At last she made herself enter the room he had borrowed from Sandry. Moonstream had taken his magical possessions and journal for examination, but his clothes and books were still there. Like Briar, she could see that Aymery spared no expense on himself. No wonder he'd had debts—debts the pirate mage had used to get him into his power. What was his name? Enahar? He had bought a Chandler like a toy, used him until he tired of it, then thrown the toy away. She reflected on these things, rubbing the ear-ring with her thumb.

"Merchant girl, you have *got* to pull yourself in and stop this foolishness," Daja said from behind her.

Tris stared at her. "Foolishness?" she asked numbly.

Daja pointed. "Your dress is starting to smoke. There's sparks jumping all over you."

Tris looked down. There *were* scorch marks on her clothes. "I'm all right," she said, and went to check the porridge.

Daja leaned back when she passed. "All right as compared to what?"

"Let me be," Tris advised, stirring the pot. "My feelings are none of your affair."

Daja fixed tea. "They are if you burn this house down around our ears."

"I'm not going to do that," said Tris grimly, the ends of her hair gleaming with tiny sparks. "If I burn anything, it's going to be pirates."

"Wonderful. How?"

"I'll think of something."

Daja crossed her arms over her chest, staring at the other girl. "Well, if you think of something, I might help. *Might.*"

"Help what?" Yawning widely, Rosethorn came out of her room, shutting the door behind her. "Is there any tea from last night?"

"There's fresh—it just has to steep a little more," said Daja. Rosethorn nodded and lurched out the back door to the privy.

Taking her spoon from the pot, Tris faced into the draft that blew in through the open door and sniffed. The wind had risen and changed, coming now out of the south. It was prodding the fog. Reaching out with her mind, she found a tiny bit of magic in it, something as faint as the scent in a long-dried rose. "Wind's turning," she whispered. "It'll blow off the fog."

Daja frowned. She didn't like the sound of that.

"It's almost like there's magic in it, but it feels really strange," Tris added.

There were no odd sparks playing over Tris's skin or hair now, no small lightning bolts playing across the spaces between her fingers. Hesitantly, Daja rested a hand on the other girl's shoulder, expecting a shock. She was relieved when it didn't come.

The contact brought their magics together. She saw what Tris meant. She could even guess the explanation. "I think maybe some people untied a *bijili*-knot," she whispered. "One that *mimanders* tied south winds into. It *feels* like *mimander*-work, anyway."

"So you Traders really *will* sell to anyone, won't you?" growled Tris, yanking out of Daja's hold. "Even filthy *jishen*."

"I don't hear you when you cluck like a *kaq*," Daja replied coolly. "And I doubt it. Dealing with pirates gets you executed by your own crew. I bet they took the *bijili* from Traders they killed."

Tris started to argue, then let the harsh words go. Daja was probably right. Why pay money when you can take from the dead?

A screech burst out of the covered nest on the table. Her charge was ready to eat again. Rosethorn,

194

coming back from the privy, stuffed her fingers into her ears and retreated to her room.

No one kept the schedule that morning, but the chores got done. When Briar had finished the breakfast dishes, Rosethorn took him to view the greenery around the north gate, with an eye to fixing the damage from the hailstorm. She was careful not to look at Tris when she mentioned it, but the girl blushed and shrunk in on herself anyway. In daylight, she could see bruises on everyone, even herself, marking the areas they hadn't been able to protect from the tumbling ice-chips.

"I didn't *mean* to create hail," she muttered to Daja and Frostpine as she settled at the table. They were putting out the things they would need to work on the spell-net: coils of wire, bits of mirror with metal loops on the back, pieces of the old spell-net, pliers.

"It did a good thing," Frostpine pointed out. "It slowed the pirates down and helped those who were drugged to wake up. It probably saved our people's lives, and yours. See how this works, Daja? Use the wire to create new squares of net. Start with the edges of the old net and build out from it. For the plain joinings, where you aren't putting a mirror, just twist the strands around each other three times. Where you want to put a mirror—" He showed her how to do it, giving two metal strands one twist around each other, threading one through the loop on back of each mirror, and giving them another twist.

"I have to inspect the gate," he said when it was clear that Daja had gotten the knack of net-mending. "They'll need all new metal work for that, I'm afraid. You girls stay put," he added as Sandry emerged from Lark's workshop, carrying her small loom. "Don't leave this cottage for any reason, unless it's with permission from an adult." Frostpine picked up the tool-box that Kirel had sent over the day before. Smiling ruefully, he told Tris, "About your hail. I'm not saying it would be terrible if you could learn—once you got a wind or a storm going—how to send it someplace in particular. Seems to me that if air and water get all stirred up when you do, they might want to listen to you as well. You just have to be firm with them." He waved and left the cottage.

Tris slumped on the table, her chin on her hands, staring into space as Daja and Sandry worked. "Easy for him to say," she commented.

"I've seen him call a rope of forge-fire over to re-heat small pieces of metal," Daja remarked. "It's much the same, only he already has to have a fire burning. You get winds to come out of nowhere."

Being firm with winds and such, Tris thought, walking over to the stone jars where things like flour and spices were kept. What's the point?

It's worth a *try*, argued another part of herself. *Anything* is better than thinking about Aymery and that awful soggy patch on his chest.

Using a tiny spoon, she carried flour back to the

table and dumped it in a heap in front of her chair. "Don't watch," she told the other girls. "It'll probably go wrong." Daja and Sandry nodded and worked at their tasks.

Sitting, Tris propped her chin on her hands, looking at the flour. Taking a deep breath, she searched the air for a breeze and found one, jumping in and out of the cottage at the back door. She snatched a pinch of it and pulled it over to the table. Feeling it wriggle eel-like in her magical grip, she squeezed until it went still, then placed it over the flour.

Reaching out with one finger, she stirred her captured breeze. It began to spin.

Keep going, Tris ordered it, and gave her finger another twirl.

The breeze reached into the flour, drawing it up as it spun. Now it could be seen, a thin cone of white that whirled like a top, its point set firmly in a shrinking mound of flour. At last Tris flicked all of her fingers at it, pushing it across her end of the table, away from Daja and Sandry, until it reached the edge. With a twitch of the hand, Tris called it back. It spun in front of her briefly, then collapsed, leaving a spray of powder as its remains.

"Maybe a bigger wind holds the shape longer?" Tris asked, thinking aloud. Reaching out, she found a larger breeze and called it. She worked up a sweat, making flour whirlwinds, but she also kept them on the table, away from her friends. That was a start, at least. She finally stopped fooling with the air when her nestling informed her—informed everyone—that he was ready for another meal.

An hour after midday Tris checked the fog. It was almost gone, shredded by the winds from the cove. Her fingers had rediscovered Aymery's earring in her pocket and were rolling it around and around in her hand. Magic ought to be simple, she thought. You create an illusion, and it ought to last until you uncreate it. You call up fog, and it should stay where you want it until you don't need it anymore.

But *anyone* can play with magic, can't they? If they can't undo the fog, they can turn up something to blow it away. They'll use battlefire to kill the wall of thorns, once they can see to launch it again, and they'll use boom-stones to destroy the spell-net, taking the protections off the rest of Winding Circle. And then they'll come in.

"Start killing," the ugly pirate had said. That was what awaited them—that or slavery.

"I wish I could do it like you," Daja told Sandry in disgust as Tris returned. The Trader put her pliers down. "It would be so easy." Taking lengths of wire, she laid them on the table in straight lines and began to weave a fresh strand through them, under one wire and over the next, as Sandry giggled. She did four rows that way, until she had a neat checkerboard of copper, silver, and gold strands on the table before her.

"Wait," Tris said as Daja was about to sweep the

design away. "Wait a moment." Frowning, she sat back and held up her hand. Thinking about Aymery had upset her again. The lightning had come back; she could see it flicker as her hair fluffed up. Now a spark shimmered between her thumb and forefinger, growing larger under her stare. It drifted left. The moment it touched her forefinger, it jumped to her thumb, leaving a bright trail behind it. The trail flickered, rippled, and stayed. A miniature lightning bolt now played between Tris's fingers.

She walked around the table to stand in front of Daja's work, not seeing that Daja moved away from her. Bending down, Tris held the tiny bolt over the point where a wire passed under another.

"Strike," murmured Tris, drawing on her magic. She pointed, just as she had with the small whirlwinds. The lightning was more difficult to handle; it kept trying to jump free of her control.

"Strike," she ordered, forcing her power onto the small strip.

The bolt flared and lashed so fast that none of them could trace its path. It struck the table, leaving a deep scorch mark.

Tris bit her lower lip and called up a new flake of lightning. This one was quicker to grow from its seed-spark. "Strike," she ordered, focusing her mind on the join of two wires.

It struck. A nearby piece of mirror cracked and blackened.

"Tris—" Daja said.

Sandry put her hand on Daja's arm, hushing her. Tris called a third bit of lightning out of the sparks that rippled over her hair. "Strike." She bore down even harder with her mind, her will, and her magic.

The strip reached across the space between her hand and the crossed wires. For a breath it hovered as if it were unsure. Then it leaped, arrowing into the space where the wires touched. There was a crackle and a smell of hot copper. Tris moved back with a sigh as Daja bent in to look.

"Oti, log this," Daja whispered to the Trader goddess. The pair of wires were fused as neatly as if she had pressed hot iron against them. Sandry clapped.

All of her sparks had died in her glee over her success, but Tris had an idea. In making them big enough to act like real lightning bolts, she had gotten a better sense of her power and theirs. Tasting lightning, she knew it to the marrow of her bones and could summon more. She did so three more times, melting Daja's wires together in three more places, so they formed without Daja twisting them together.

Lark, Frostpine, Briar, and Rosethorn returned as the girls were starting a late midday. Everyone was glad to sit and eat. The adults passed on the information that the north gate was closed and being rebuilt, while the spell-nets now hid Winding Circle in the north as well as the east and west. There would be no more attacks from that direction, or so everyone had to hope. No one mentioned what would happen if the pirates were able to blast the buried spell-nets to pieces with boom-stones.

Niko arrived as they were finishing. To everyone's surprise and delight, Dedicate Gorse was with him. The stocky kitchen dedicate had brought a batch of fried sweet cakes for them to try out and fresh ground meat and egg yolks for the nestling. He watched as Tris prepared the balls of meat-and-egg paste and even tried his hand at stuffing two into the starling's maw.

"If we're ready?" Niko asked when the bird had settled to sleep again.

Gorse looked up at him and nodded.

"Children, I want each of you to stand behind your teacher," Niko said. "We're going to conduct some experiments." He placed a leather bag the size of a cabbage on the table.

"What kind of experiments?" asked Rosethorn suspiciously.

Niko very carefully poured a spoonful of grainy black dust out of the bag. "We got this from the prisoners," he explained. "It's what they used to shatter the gate, and it's what they use in the boom-stones. They just call it black powder. Its ingredients and the proportions are the pirate mage Enahar's secret. That's what we have to find out."

"Surely Moonstream and Skyfire—" Lark began.

"They want all the masters to try it," Niko said.

"That way, everyone will have a working knowledge of the stuff. Now, dedicates, if we may begin?"

All five adults reached a hand out to the tiny pile, palms toward it, eyes closed; when they took deep breaths, clearing their minds, the four did the same.

"Charcoal," Rosethorn and Frostpine announced at the same time.

Niko added, "Sulfur."

"Niter," Gorse told them, and Rosethorn nodded.

I couldn't have done it so fast, Daja remarked silently to the other children. They nodded, agreeing.

The adults argued for half an hour over the proportions of each substance. At last they managed to agree: ten parts sulfur, fifteen parts charcoal, and seventy-five parts niter.

"It's so basic!" Lark said then. "So—so simple! And it won't take much to make it explode, once you get through the protections on the containers."

"Which is *why* the containers have been so well protected magically," added Frostpine.

"But what makes it boom?" Daja asked, worried. "What if it—?"

A crash split the air outside, making everyone flinch. Seconds later, they heard another loud bang, from the eastern side of the temple.

"They've started again," whispered Daja. Tris was trembling.

"Let's go outside," Niko said, brushing the spoonful

into the bag. "We can try to make it boom there. Fire does the trick, if what Tris and I saw on Bit was right."

In front of Discipline, on a bare spot in the path, Niko dumped a pinch of the black powder on the ground. Someone brought a long, burning reed, and Niko touched the powder with it from a couple of feet away. As a boom-stone exploded over the south half of the temple, the tiny heap of powder flared and was consumed.

"They have to leave a gap in the spells on the containers," Rosethorn pointed out, "so their mages can light the stones in the air."

"Will our battle-mages find the gaps in time to explode the stones before they get too close to us?" Frostpine wanted to know.

Niko poured half a cupful of powder onto the path, then wiped his forehead with one hand, leaving a dark streak. "Everybody stand back when I light this." He held the reed out to Gorse, who touched it with a finger. Flames leaped and caught on the tip of the reed.

"But the little sample just burned," Lark said. "How do they make it boom?"

"Perhaps you need more?" suggested Rosethorn as everyone backed away from the larger pile. "Or it has to be confined, in a sphere or—"

The loudest explosion of all tore the air, making everyone stagger. The adults looked at each other, horrified, then turned their eyes on the horizon. A column of smoke boiled into the air south of the Water Temple.

"One of them hit," Lark whispered.

Rosethorn raced into the cottage. Briar followed her.

"The carpenters' shops," said Gorse, his deep voice hushed. "All that wood—the glue, the varnishes—"

"It'll burn fast and hot." Frostpine made the gods-circle on his chest.

Tris was shaking so hard that her teeth were clicking. Where would the next stone fall? The image of the destroyed galley rose in her mind, a warning of the fate of anything struck by these ugly new weapons.

Lark turned to the four. "You are to stay *right here.*" They had never heard her this stern. "Don't stir outside our fence. We're going down there to help. I don't want to have to worry about what *you're* up to."

"Can't we help?" begged Sandry.

"No. No. There are plenty of adults trained to handle things like this. I won't have you exposed unless it can't be avoided."

Rosethorn came out, lugging a heavy basket. Briar followed her with another. "Can't I *please* go?" he asked as Frostpine took his burden.

"*No,* you may *not,*" snapped Rosethorn. "You'll stay here—all of you!"

Without another word, the adults ran through the

gate and down the spiral road. Little Bear sat on his rump and began to howl.

Three more boom-stones exploded overhead. Tris flinched at each one; her hair began to rise and crackle. She tucked her hand into her pocket and rubbed Aymery's earring.

They had to distract Tris before something else happened, thought Daja. "What if you tried your lightning on that?" She pointed to the heap of black powder that lay forgotten in the path.

Tris stared at it. "I—I don't know," she said, her voice trembling.

"Well?" Sandry nudged.

"What lightning?" Briar demanded, sarcastic. "She's just got the worst case of Runog's Fire I've ever seen, is all."

Daja knew the pale fire that played on ship masts and tower roofs in storms as well as he did. "What she's *got* is seed lightning," she retorted. "It's not the same. Show him, Tris."

Another boom-stone exploded over the Hub. "I c-c-can't," Tris replied, shivering with fright. What did they want from her? Couldn't they see that each explosion felt like a sharp blow to her? Her muscles were clenched, awaiting the next strike, and her neck and back were aching.

"Don't you have to learn control?" Sandry asked. "No matter what else is going on? Maybe this is a good time to practice."

Tris glared at the other three, hating them for bothering her. She only wanted to run inside and hide under a bed.

"Ahhh, I knew it," Briar remarked scornfully. "It's just Runog's Fire."

Furious, Tris pointed to the heap of powder a foot away. Lightning jumped from her finger. There was a clap: dirt and smoke sprayed everywhere, blackening them and turning the observing Little Bear gray. The dog yipped and fled into Discipline. The four looked at each other, eyes wide in soot-streaked faces. There was now a hole in the path.

"You see?" Briar said at last. "You just have to know what to say to her."

"You—" Tris snapped, and pointed at him without thinking what might result.

Briar grabbed her arms, hard, shaking her as lightning-sparks raced over his hands. "Don't you *ever* do that," he whispered, his eyes burning into hers. "Don't you *ever*. If your pointing is a weapon, then don't you point 'less you're ready to kill with it. You understand, you witless bleater?" He was so frightened he didn't know where his shakes ended and hers began. "Niko's right." He let her go and pushed her away from him. "We've *got* to learn control, and *you* most of all."

"I'm sorry." Tris's eyes were spilling over, but she made herself look Briar in the face. "I'm sorry. I didn't—I wouldn't ever—"

Sandry put her arms around Tris's shoulders. "We can't just act without thinking anymore, Tris. They've been trying to teach us that all along. I guess if we're mages, we can't exactly be kids, can we?" she asked the other two. They shook their heads. "Briar knows you would have been sorry after."

"After I was a nice crispy roast just off the spit," the boy said cruelly.

Tris hid her face in her hands.

"Enough," Daja said. "She got the point. Don't bully her."

I'm a *scared* bully, thought Briar, stuffing his hands into his pockets. And I want to be sure *she's* scared, scared enough to think next time.

Tris yanked out of Sandry's hold and ran up to her room.

Briar went to examine the miniature pine tree that sat on his window ledge, letting the *shakkan*'s years and plant-calm steady his nerves. Checking the dirt in its shallow basin, he decided it was a bit dry and went inside for water.

Daja and Sandry stayed where they were, staring at the hole in the ground.

"What do you suppose her reach is, with lightning?" Daja inquired. "Could she hit a boom-stone?"

Sandry tugged one of her braids. "I don't know. Remember the day we all first met? Lightning struck a tree outside Administration when we were there. I think that was her—she was angry; I could tell the moment I laid eyes on her. And she wasn't excited by lightning hitting so close to her. But it was stormy that morning. This lightning just seems to cling to her—it's not part of a storm. It might not reach as far."

"But when she holds onto it, it grows. Remember? It starts as a spark. Then she holds it, and it grows into a strip." Daja scuffed at the dirt around the hole.

"*I* think we should find out how far she can send it." Sandry bent down and petted Little Bear, who had crept out of the house again.

"I think you're right," said Daja.

The safest place looked to be the lee of the northern wall beside Discipline. There was a broad strip of grass with no other plants growing on it—Briar had refused to allow an experiment anywhere in Rosethorn's garden. Only the sentries could see them, but for the most part they were looking to the north, or the south, where the fire was. By now the word had come up the road: a boom-stone had gotten through the magical barriers, exploding in one of the large buildings that housed Winding Circle's carpentry shops. There were dead and wounded and people trapped inside. It would be a while before their teachers could be spared from rescue work.

Once Briar had been converted to the idea of lightning experiments, he made some reed circles for use as targets. Sandry dug in Lark's scrap bag and brought out a number of cloth patches that she placed in different spots. Daja's job was to get Tris to go along.

"I think this is stupid," Tris informed them when Daja brought her to the spot they'd prepared. "I can only do it when I'm upset."

"It's magic; it's there all the time," Briar told her impatiently. "Stop it with the ladylike whining. 'Oh, I can't; I have to be *scared.*'"

Tris glared at him. "Why can't you let me alone?"

"Because I'm tired of living with a merchant sniffer!" he told her. "Rosethorn's out there putting healing in potions, and she's been doing it ever since the quake—"

Tris pointed at a swatch of cloth two feet away. Lightning stretched across the gap between her and the path, but didn't touch it.

"You need me to go on carping?" Briar asked. "I've got plenty more to say—"

"You aren't always fun to live with, either, you know!" Tris snapped. She called the lightning back. For a moment she stood very still, eyes closed, breathing deep. She pointed again.

The bolt left a scorch mark on the cloth.

"Got to do better than that," said Daja, shaking her head.

"I'd like to see *you* try," muttered Tris. She wrapped her free hand around Aymery's earring and pointed. The patch evaporated in a plume of smoke.

"I shouldn't have used silk," whispered Sandry. "It goes up *so* fast."

Tris pointed to the wall, five feet in front of her, where another patch was fastened to a chink in the mortar with a thorn. Lightning stretched across the distance, but only halfway.

"Something closer," said Daja. She tossed a cloth patch several inches beyond where the first had been.

An hour later there were scorch marks on the wall, and Tris had to feed her nestling. When she returned, she brought him with her and gave his nest to Sandry to hold. "He's supposed to be kept quiet," she said. "I guess there's no chance of that now." The boom-stones had been exploding overhead off and on all afternoon.

Sandry peeked at the bird and stopped Little Bear from trying the same thing. "He looks all right," she told Tris. "He's not shaking. I keep meaning to ask, what have you got in your pocket? You keep fiddling with something."

Grimly Tris held up Aymery's earring. "It helps me concentrate."

Sandry turned her head to order Little Bear to stop chewing on grass and stopped. Light flickered at the corner of her eye, light that was not one of the other children. "That earring is magicked," she said, shocked. "And what's that thread coming out of it?"

Tris looked sidelong at it. "You're right about the

magic. Aymery told me the pirate mage created it, as a bond to enslave him. I don't see a thread, though."

"It's there, heading off"— Sandry pointed due south— "that way."

Daja squinted at the earring. "I see a ghost of a wire," she admitted. "But I never noticed it before. Just that blasted flickering."

"Blame Niko," protested Tris. "I never thought that seeing-spell would cross between us like it does."

"I bet the thread is the magical bond. It goes to that mage—Enahar? Stupid name," said Briar. "Too bad we couldn't send him a little lightning, by way of it."

"It would have to go through buildings and the wall," Daja pointed out. "I don't believe it would get there."

"Let's try something more fun," Briar said, holding up a reed circle. "Tris, get one of these while they're in the air."

"You've *got* to be joking." Shaking her head, Tris planted her feet wide apart, to give her the best possible stance. As she gripped Aymery's earring, sparks began to glimmer in her tumbling curls. "All right, Briar, but I still don't think I can do it."

Briar tossed a reed circle into the air. Tris pointed, but the lightning on her fingertip tangled, writhing around her hand like knotted string. Briar threw again, lower. This time the lightning missed by a hair. He threw a third time, and Little Bear jumped,

211

grabbing the circle in his teeth. Tris burned a streak on the wall, keeping the lighting away from the pup.

"I can't do this!" she cried, out of patience. "It's like playing with poison! It—"

Daja gasped, pointing at the sky. High overhead, a small, round shape had begun to fall toward them.

A blazing strip of white heat roared past them. It struck the boom-stone, blowing it to pieces two hundred feet overhead. The children hid their faces as soot and pottery fragments rained down on them.

Tris wobbled. Her knees gave, and she sat down hard. Little Bear came to lick her cheek. The other three children turned to stare at her.

"I guess we just need to make it worth your while," remarked Daja.

12

Taking supper from the cart sent up from the Hub and putting it on the table, the four were wondering if they would have to eat alone when their teachers returned. The adults had obviously bathed in the Water Temple baths before coming on to Discipline: all wore undyed robes and carried their own clothes in string bags. The bags were left near the back door. Sandry, looking at the garments, wondered if they could even be used for rags, as sooty, torn, and scorched as they were. The smell that rose from them was vile and made her queasy.

The adults spoke little and ate less. There seemed

to be no way to mention controlled lightning after the first few "Not nows" the four got. Instead of following the chore schedule, they were sent to the Earth Temple baths, while the adults cleaned up. When the children came back, they went quietly to their rooms, to read or think.

They all slept badly. When Tris cried, the other three knew it. When Briar dreamed of starving and watching the bread he'd just snatched melt through his fingers, they knew it. When dawn came, they were roused not by the Hub clock, but by the first boom-stone explosion of the day.

Everyone was up after that. Like the night before, no one spoke much. Tris fed her nestling, barely smiling when Rosethorn pointed out that nearly all of his gray pinfeathers had come in. He might be ready to fly in another two weeks.

"Into a boom-stone," Briar growled.

"Enough of that," instructed Niko.

Breakfast was over when Moonstream and Skyfire arrived, looking as if they had spent as good a night as those at Discipline had. "We need to talk," Moonstream said after she kissed Niko's cheek. She looked meaningfully at the children.

"Upstairs," Rosethorn ordered.

They started to argue. Niko said sharply, *"Now."*

"Just like Mother in her captain mood," Daja remarked mournfully. Gathering up dog and starling, they climbed the steep ladder-stair.

"They're treating us like children," Sandry commented rebelliously as the four sat on the floor around the topmost step.

"We *are* kids," Briar reminded her.

"But if we're mages, are we kids?" demanded Tris.

Frostpine appeared at the bottom of the stairs. "We would appreciate it if you would go into one of the rooms and *not* eavesdrop." His dark eyes were bloodshot and level, with no hint of his usual laughter in them. "Scat."

Grumbling, they obeyed. Tris hung back, shooing the others into her room. Making sure Frostpine had left the steps, she reached through the opening in the floor to grab a fistful of air from downstairs. Carefully she backed into her room, letting it out of her fingers a breath at a time. Once inside, she drew the breeze over to her window and sent it out that way. Now she had a steady draft coming from the ground floor.

"What—?" Briar started to ask.

Tris put a finger to her lips and cupped a hand around her ear.

"*—used battlefire on the thorns late yesterday,*" Skyfire was saying. "*They're pounding the spell-net in the east with the black powder balls. Those things make a deep hole when they strike the ground—they're blowing the spell-net apart, working their way in. Two more days, and they'll be at the east gate. And even though we've found out how their black powder works, there's no guarantee some boom-stones won't get past our mages. They'll*

215

throw as many as they can over our walls, to soften us up. Some are bound to hit."

"Have the war-mages been able to get through the protective barrier around the pirate fleet?" Rosethorn wanted to know.

"They've thrown all they have at that cursed thing— nothing gets through," Skyfire replied bitterly. *"Water-mages say it goes to the floor of the sea."*

"He's got the barrier salted with mage-traps." That was Niko. *"He really likes to use other mages' power in his work, this Enahar."*

The four looked at each other and moved closer together, for comfort.

"What of the navy?" Lark wanted to know.

"No word, the duke says," Moonstream told them. *"They may come, they may not. You need to evacuate the children. We can take them to Summersea through the hidden ways. A load of the worst sick and injured are going at noon."*

"No!" cried Sandry, eyes blazing. "Absolutely not!"

Tris and Daja shushed her. From below Niko called, "What's going on up there?"

Briar went to the door. "We're just frisking like little captive lambkins."

There was a crack of laughter from downstairs: Skyfire, perhaps.

"Frisk quietly," Rosethorn ordered.

Briar stepped back into the room.

"They are *not* sending me to my uncle!" Sandry

thrust her chin out as far as it would go. "I won't leave!"

"Is that what 'evacuating' means?" the boy inquired.

"That's what it means," Daja replied.

Tris's face was dead white. Small lightnings crackled all over her hair and dress. Winds stirred in every corner of the room. "They can't send me away again. They *can't*."

Another boom-stone exploded in midair. Tris flinched.

"It'll get you away from *that*," pointed out Daja.

"And what'll be here when we come back?" Briar wanted to know.

None of them could answer.

"Pirates killed my favorite cousin. Now they're going to drive me from the only place I ever felt welcome," Tris said very softly. "I'm done with being pushed around by the likes of them!" Going to the window, she sat on the ledge, and swung her legs outside. She would go up on the wall, she decided, and throw lightning at them until it killed her.

Sandry lunged and grabbed her. The lightnings prickled, but didn't hurt.

"Let me *go!*" snarled Tris, fighting. Daja came over to help.

"Listen to me. *Listen!*" Sandry talked low and fast, trying to hold Tris's attention. "You want to fight back, and that makes perfect sense, but you can't do it by yourself. Haven't we all been hurt? This is our home, too, the best we've ever had." Tris was still trying to wriggle out of their hold. "You need our help. Listen to me, are you listening?"

The roar of a boom-stone shook the rafters.

"Let me go," panted Tris.

"She's right," Daja insisted, dragging her inside. "Listen to her."

All three girls tumbled onto the floor with a thud. Sandry's and Daja's hair fought to rise out of their braids.

Briar listened at the door. The adults seemed to be too deep into their talk to pay attention to them. "We won't be allowed on the wall," he pointed out.

"We don't need their permission," Sandry replied. She had given up on reasoning with Tris and was now sitting on the redhead's stomach. "Remember the other night? How we protected ourselves at the north gate? *I* can do that. I can keep anyone from touching us. I don't want to go! If the pirates took this place— if they hurt Lark—"

She looked away, blinking eyes that stung. The lightnings had slowed down, but now they climbed on her and Daja just as they did on Tris.

Must be more light than heat, Briar thought, looking at the girls. And isn't that just as well? Or Tris'd cook anyone who came near her.

"I don't think I could bear it, if Winding Circle fell," murmured Daja. "I can be a bellows and blow people away from us. Or—or I think—I think . . ." She halted, turning something over in her mind.

"Let me up," said Tris. "I won't climb out the window."

"Promise?" asked Sandry.

"Promise."

Sandry and Daja rose to their feet. Little Bear got in a few licks before Tris could stand and take her face away from his tongue.

Briar eyed Tris suspiciously. He didn't like the stubborn set of her mouth. Her lightnings seemed thicker; so did her hair. "You look like a bush," he informed her.

Tris grumbled. Seizing a long scarf, she wrapped it around her head and tied it tightly. Past the cloth her curls still rose to fan out, but at least she didn't look so odd.

"What about their magic barrier?" she asked, sitting on the bed. "You heard Skyfire."

"We can ram through," Daja said. "They're always telling us how much stronger we are when we hook up. I wish we had the string, though."

"You sure we need it?" Briar inquired. "We did all right at north gate. Maybe we just *thought* we had to touch it."

"I have to use the privy," Tris announced. "I had too much juice."

"If they'll let you down there," Briar said.

Tris smoothed her skirts. Her lightnings had faded.

"I have to *go*. I'll be right back. Don't make plans without me. I want to get these—*jishen*." She brushed past him and trotted downstairs.

"If Sandry protects us, and if I get near the ships, well . . ." Daja mused.

"Tell us," Sandry urged.

"When Frostpine and I did the harbor chain, he made the chain rise in the air. I'm *pretty* sure I remember how." It was one of many things burned into her mind when they had magicked the chain so hard and so fast. "I think I can get metal to pull out of whatever it's attached to, in a small area. Maybe even drag nails from their moorings."

"I'll find something to do," said Briar. "There's always getting seaweed to foul their oars. And if Coppercurls can use her lightning, we might be able to make these turd-eaters back off."

They discussed their plans for a few more minutes. Briar was the first to realize that, for someone who promised to be right back, Tris was taking a very long time.

"Wait here," he told the other two. He swung out of the window, letting himself drop to the pillows on the roof of Rosethorn's shop, where Tris had planned to fall. He landed with little more than a bump, just as another boom-stone exploded. Carefully he dropped to the ground. They waited nervously as he trotted around to the privy. Within moments he was back, scowling furiously.

She's gone! he mouthed.

"Help me down," Sandry told Daja, tucking her skirts between her knees. She sat on the windowsill and swung her legs outside. Daja lowered her as much as she could until Sandry was able to drop lightly to the workshop roof. On her jump to the ground, Briar was there to catch her.

Daja wasn't about to risk the thump the adults would hear if she dropped. Running into the attic, she got a coil of rope. With a few quick twists, she secured one end to Tris's bed. Clinging to the rope, she lowered herself to the ground.

"Where would she go?" Briar asked when Daja arrived. They trotted away from the house, coming out of the gardens and onto the grassy strip on the inside of the wall. "There's sentries all over the wall."

From the cottage behind them, they heard the first bark. Little Bear did not like to be left behind.

"Maybe she'll keep them off with lightning, or the wind," Daja said. "You know how she is. They might not know the lightning she wears doesn't hurt."

"Wait," Sandry told them. She closed her eyes and held out her hand, palm-up, wriggling her fingers. "I feel your thread, Daja, and Briar's . . ." She closed her hand and opened her eyes. "She's headed for the south wall, for certain." As they began to run again, she added, "Maybe the lightning only just tickles us because, well—"

"Her magic bleeds into ours," said Briar. "So maybe

it thinks we're part of her? I hope she thinks of that before she scorches anyone who *isn't* part of her."

"When I catch her, I am going to give her a pounding," threatened Daja. "She is the most aggravating girl I ever met—apart from you," she told Sandry.

"How long before they see we're gone?" asked Briar. "Not too, if Little Bear keeps it up." They ran faster.

Tris did not run—she was too fat, and it would be silly to reach the wall too winded to climb to the top. She walked quickly; her friends might just follow. Tramping through the grass beside the wall, she worked her feelings to a fever pitch. Emotions were the key to her power to damage things, weren't they? She remembered her parents' faces when they told a perfect stranger at Stone Circle Temple that they no longer wanted her. She remembered Uraelle taking her books when the chores weren't done as well as she demanded, and dormitory girls taunting her about her looks. She remembered Winding Circle boys who called her "fatty" and made pig noises at her.

The winds came to her, whipping her clothes and wrestling the lightning for her hair. They tugged her this way and that as she mounted the stairs a few hundred yards from the south gate.

"Get out of here!" cried a guard, running toward her. "It's not safe!"

A billow of wind struck his chest, knocking him

down. "Stay back," Tris warned. "I don't want to hurt you."

He got up and advanced. She sent the wind at him again, strengthening it. It pinned him to the wall. Glancing to either side, Tris saw more guards take notice. They were coming to their comrade's help. Behind them, further down the wall, mages were looking to see what the trouble was.

She had to keep everyone off her. Using winds on them cost her little; she only needed a dab of magic to send them where she wanted, since the winds were already here. Working them was distracting, though, and she couldn't afford distractions.

Once Niko had told the four that, when things were difficult, they could open their minds and let the magic guide them. Tris did so now, looking to see how she could work uninterrupted.

The image of a circle bloomed against her closed eyelids. Rosethorn and Lark had created magical circles before, to keep magic in. Who was to say they couldn't be used to keep people out?

She dragged her fingers through her hair, collecting a palmful of sparks. A quick glance around told her the mages were now advancing with the guards. Swiftly she worked the sparks with her free hand, ignoring the needlelike pricks the bits of lightning gave her as she shaped them. Pointing to the walkway before her with the hand that held the ball of sparks, Tris began to turn, drawing a circle of lightning. Its fire streamed down, burning where she placed it, until she closed the circle. She was now fully enclosed, with a good two feet of room on either side. Twitching her fingers, she raised the fiery circle until it made a wall over five feet high at her back and sides. Before her lay the top of the wall and the cove. *Now* she could get to work.

Tris grabbed two fistfuls of wind. She twisted them around each other, following the lessons taught by Lark and Sandry: spinning made weak fibers into strong thread. Finished, she backed up to the inner edge of her lightning-circle and stood her wind-thread at its center. Grimly, she twirled her finger clockwise. The wind began to whirl.

Bit by bit it drew in pieces of other winds, growing taller and wider. When it was of a size to crowd Tris out of the circle, she sent it into the air and let it touch down in the blanket of thorns on the other side of the wall. Twigs and sticks fought their way up the growing funnel as it ate vines, becoming a thorny kind of armor.

Once Tris had fought, and failed, to make a water-funnel do as she wanted, and it had been only ten feet tall. Now when her cyclone towered thirty feet in the air, higher than the wall on which she stood, she urged it up, out of the brambles. Making shooing motions with her hands, she sent it forward.

The moment it entered the sea, the funnel turned into a waterspout. It widened and continued to grow as it bore down on the pirate fleet. Ten yards or so from the closest galley, the waterspout struck the pirates' magical barrier and stopped.

"Aymery," she growled to make herself angrier, and slammed her creation forward. It sprayed against the glasslike wall, grinding at it. "Aymery, and the carpenters, and your poor slaves." Again and again she threw her creation at the barrier, without result.

"Now you know why you need *us*." Sandry walked through the lightning-wall to stare reproachfully at Tris. "You should have waited."

Soldiers and mages clustered at a respectful distance from Tris's fiery hideout. It was easy for the other three to see who had gone closest to it: their hair stood on end. Daja nodded gravely to them as she and Briar followed Sandry through the lightning.

Tris stared at them, baffled. "It didn't hurt you?"

"It stings," said Daja, rubbing her arms.

Briar took a place at Tris's side. "You can't pound pirates without us," he told her. "It wouldn't be as much fun."

"They'll know we're gone soon," pointed out Sandry. All four knew who "they" were. "We need more than this circle to keep them from stopping us."

"This was the best I could do." Tris sent more winds out to help the waterspout and smiled as the funnel got longer and fatter still.

"But *we* can do better," Sandry informed her. "Why not take this circle up, and I'll weave us a new one?"

"New one first," said Daja. "Then break the old one. Otherwise those guards outside will grab us."

Sandry nodded. Laying her palms flat against the lightning barrier, ignoring the pain as its fire bit into her skin, she searched her mind for the wall that had kept them safe at the north gate. Thread by thread she wove it against the lightning's surface, her magic shuttling faster than the eye could follow. Her barrier rose around the four, holding the same shape as the lightning wall.

When it was complete, she took her hands away. "It'll be stronger when we join," she told her companions.

Tris closed her eyes, calling to her original protection. The lightning poured over Sandry's wall in a stream of white heat to pool in the redhead's cupped palms. When she had retrieved all of it, she rolled it into a fiery ball and put it on the wall in front of them.

Closing their eyes, the four joined as they had once done in the middle of an earthquake, to become one. Daja was not sure that she liked such closeness. Briar felt the same way. Sandry brushed them with soothing warmth, reminding them that it was just for the moment, then turned her attention to the moon-pale wall that she had built. Touching it with their strength, she made it blaze.

Let's get to it, Tris said.

Not so fast, replied Daja. *Weren't you listening?*

There are mage-traps in the barrier. If we attack it, let's make sure we don't strike one.

We don't even know what they look like, Sandry argued.

Just look at it, Briar told her. *We've been seeing magic for days. Let's find out if we can spot differences in the stuff.*

Leaving their bodies on the wall, the four went to the magical shield. Sandry hunted for changes in its weave, Tris for storm centers, Daja for rust spots. From his long experience in climbing garden and house walls, Briar knew better than to trust his eyes: Bags always paid extra for spells to hide other spells. Flinging his mind forward, the ex-thief went over the silvery wall an inch at a time, poking it with a finger.

Here, he said at last. *And here, and here.*

We don't have to look more, Tris pointed out. *If we hit the barrier in the middle of those spots, we might break through.*

Let your waterspout spin us together, Daja suggested. *To make us stronger. When we come out through the top, we'll fly at that place.*

Briar left a dab of green fire to mark their target. The four drifted to the top lip of the waterspout as it whirled before the pirates' barrier.

Looking at the funnel, Briar said approvingly, *You've got a monster this time, Coppercurls.*

Let's go! Tris cried and let herself fall into the outside of the spout. The others followed, wrapping themselves around her. The floods that whipped along the funnel's sides grabbed them, twirling them around and around as wind and water carried them down to the sea. They could feel themselves being wound ever more tightly into one being.

Daja felt heat as well, the heat of a forge-fire, warming them, making them blend together easily. How much more of their power would leak between them if they survived this? There was no chance to really consider it—they rushed madly into the pointed end of the funnel and were sucked inside. Now the current bore them up through the spout, speeding them along.

Just a bit more, thought Tris as they neared the top. *A little more, a little . . .*

They shot out of the spout's top and slammed into the barrier at eyeblink speed. Something before them gave. The barrier's magic no longer felt like a smooth and solid whole.

Again, decreed Sandry.

They returned to the waterspout, soaring into its outside current and letting it yank them down. It, too, was spinning faster, twirling the four wildly. They felt powerful and furious. Shooting out of the top, they leaped away to arrow at the green spot Briar had left for them.

The whole barrier shattered like glass. In raced the waterspout. It fell on a galley in the first rank of the fleet. Chunks of wood flew as it gnawed the port oars. The four broke apart, ready to get to work.

Briar looked back. There were bare, charred patches on the shore where battlefire had roasted the brambles that he and Rosethorn had worked so hard to grow. Now a single longboat was drawn up on the blackened slope, its load of pirates already ashore. They were throwing skins of battlefire onto the remaining thorns and setting them ablaze, making room for even more invaders to land. A pair of men who glinted with magic shielded them from the spells of Winding Circle's defenders.

The boy glanced at the top of the wall. There was the glow of Sandry's protective barrier, with the four's real bodies just visible through a notch in the stone. Most of the soldiers and mages who had encircled them were gone, manning the walls and catapults against the pirates laboring on the beach. He couldn't find Skyfire's shock of red hair, but it was a long trot from Discipline to south gate. The general would be there soon, he had no doubt. Skyfire was needed; in the cove seven more longboats filled with armed pirates and their protector-mages waited for room enough to land.

Briar was not about to permit that, any more than Winding Circle's defenders were. He sank into the earth, drawing on the link between him and the girls for the power to regrow his brambles.

Daja circled a galley. Where to start? The metal of its catapult looked promising.

She thought back to that morning—just yesterday!—in the harbor. Right before Frostpine had raised the chain she had felt a thin shiver in the air, like a razor cutting a bone. She called that shiver from herself now, putting the strength of her link to the other three in it. She invited dull metal to fly.

Wood squeaked as nails fought to escape it. Weapons rose, yanking from their masters' holds. Metal fittings worked themselves off the ship and soared into the air. She drew all of it over to the ship's lee, then let the metal drop into the water. Section by section, she went over the ship, leaving ruin in her wake.

Suddenly she had to catch her breath. Opening her real eyes, Daja squinted to see through the white light of their barrier. Only a couple of soldiers remained just outside, keeping one nervous eye on the four and the other on the shore below. The south gate mages, led by Moonstream, defended the cove against a pirate landing party. Other initiates had moved into every spot along the wall that gave a view of the invaders. They knew the fleet's magical barrier was down. As Skyfire stalked to and fro on the wall, shouting orders and calling out targets, everyone who could throw fire or make ropes or chains come to life or pop lanterns from holders was at work. Invisible hands shoved raiders overboard. Oars on neighboring ships fouled one another.

A galley exploded with a roar. Someone had managed to fire its load of black powder.

Daja returned to her part of the battle. A mage with a mirror-bright brass shield was deflecting fire bolts away from his ship's catapult. She would see how long he could hold onto the shield.

When the pirates' magical wall went to pieces, Tris summoned the lightning ball that she'd left near her body on the wall. Waiting for it, she looked the fleet over. Where was Enahar? Wouldn't their boss mage—as Briar put it—be on the biggest ship? He'd be close to the pirate leader, surely.

She examined the largest galleys. Each carried men and women ablaze with inner magical fire, so that was no clue. The dromon at the center of the fleet, though, had even more mages than the others. Beneath the scarlet pennant flown by every ship was a smaller blue flag, with crossed black swords for a device. Since no one else flew two banners, she was ready to bet that was the flagship.

This is for Aymery! she cried, stretching the lightning in her hands into a long strip. *For the carpenters, and the soldier who liked dogs! This is for my starling's dead parents!* She hurled the lightning with all her might, putting her rage into it. Lengthening as it flew, it made the air boom in its wake. It struck the flagship dead center.

The ship blew up in a spray of flame and smoke. Tris flinched, though her magical body couldn't be hurt by flying debris. Burning corpses flew by, making her quail. Chunks of burning wood and red-hot metal rained down; sails caught fire. A length of flaming mast speared a lesser galley, crunching through its aftercastle. That ship exploded.

13

Tris fled back to her body. Served them right, she thought, opening her real eyes. Served them right. They're just a bunch of murdering thieves.

Reaching into her pocket, she drew out Aymery's earring. It gave off the glow of magic to her eyes. That meant Enahar was still alive. If he hadn't been on the flagship, where was he?

"Sandry?" she asked.

The other girl opened her eyes and coughed. Clouds of smoke from the brambles thickened the air around them. "Tris, that was *horrible.*"

"They wanted to do it to us," Tris pointed out.

"I know. I know, you're right." Sandry shook her head. Pirates were vermin and had to be crushed; she knew that as well as she knew her own name. It was just hard to remember when they screamed.

"Enahar wasn't there." Tris showed her the earring. "I need to find him, Sandry. This is *his* fault. He ordered Aymery killed. Help me track this thing to its source?"

Sandry nodded. Both girls closed their eyes and sent their magical selves out. They passed over a wide band of green fire, where Briar and his thorns fought landing parties for possession of the cove. Under his direction the vines lashed like whips, forcing the invaders back as the smaller thorny plants stuffed themselves into any sleeves, collars, shirttails, and breech-legs.

In the sea Tris's waterspout prowled, clipping oars, sweeping people from decks, and eating rope as it swept to and fro. A copper blaze hanging over a dromon was Daja. She had called the anchor to her and it came, rising inch by inch as it dripped seaweed and brine. Drawing it over the ship's midsection, she let it drop. It crashed through deck and hull as hard as a catapult-stone. Water fountained through the hole as the ship began to sink.

Tris looked everywhere, seeking the silver points that were mages. In places their numbers were so many that their lights joined to form a single, large blot. She kept losing the pale glimmer of the earring's thread among them.

What kind of pattern is this? Sandry wanted to know. *What's it for? It's huge, whatever it is!*

What pattern? asked Tris, confused.

You don't see it? Back on the wall, Sandry put an arm around Tris. *How about now?*

The magical Tris rose higher over the fleet. Now that she was in physical contact with Sandry, the pattern *was* clear, even with ships drifting out of line or missing entirely. Magical threads passed from mage to mage. They were thin in places where the gap was extra-large because they had lost mages, but the overall design still held.

The pattern ended in a small ship at the rear of the fleet. Other threads led away from it, to the west— toward Summersea. Tris knew that the mages in the fleet at the harbor were on the other end of those.

Sandry touched the thread of Aymery's earring, darkening it from silver to dark green, until Tris saw it clearly against all the other magics. It, too, led to that ship.

All right? asked Sandry.

Thank you, Tris replied.

On the wall, Sandry took her arm away. *Try a little mercy?* she asked, looking at the pirates and slaves who struggled in the water of the cove.

Tris raced away.

Sandry dropped, wanting a better look at the shapes created by the threads. Something was not right. She drew closer still until she hovered over a ship where three magical lines came together. Gingerly, she touched their joining.

Blackness wrapped around her eyes, her mouth, her arms. She struggled, furious, as something towed her magical self away. There was no getting free. In the distance, she felt the collapse of her protective barrier on the wall. Now anyone could approach their bodies. She could only pray that someone would, soon.

Picking a fresh dromon to work on, Daja sent her power in search of metal. Here was something else familiar: a quantity of fine charcoal, like that she and Frostpine used in the forges. Boom-dust! she thought joyfully.

This ship appeared to be a stockpile for it. She narrowed her senses until she found the door the stuff lay behind. Silver light flickered over it, but there was nothing on the metal latch. If she just opened the door and bellows-blew a lamp in there. . . . Eagerly she touched the latch.

An invisible net wrapped around her, bundling her up like a caterpillar in a cocoon. Her strength flooded from her veins. Where was her power going? What was stealing her magic? She tried to scream for the others, but her link to them was gone.

They were running at last, the scum who wanted to enslave his friends. Briar, flying through a bramble tangle, wrapped a thorny vine around one of the slower invaders. Her mates cut the woman free, dragged her aboard their longboat, and shoved off. Briar let them go. The four- and five-foot branches of seaweed growing in the cove would grab their oars. Let them sit out under the sun, without water, until they burned like his poor vines had.

He drifted among the sharp-edged plants, wondering what to do next. Something glittered, catching his eye. In the rush to escape his living needles, a pirate had dropped what looked like a gold medallion. It shimmered with a touch of magical fire. He guessed it was a protective amulet; at least, it looked like other such amulets he'd stolen. If he hid it, he could lay claim to it once the pirates were gone. He had a feeling that would be soon. Their fleet didn't look so good anymore.

Reaching down, he prodded the medallion.

A sound unpleasantly like the slam of a jail door pierced his skull. Suddenly he was locked in place, unable to move or call out for help. Worse—much, much worse—his power was racing away, draining through a handful of once-invisible threads that ran from the medallion into the fleet. His magic was fading. Without it, his plants withered. They collapsed. The way to Winding Circle was open to anyone who chose to row back, as the eight longboats were doing now.

Tris's flight toward the ship in the rear came to a smashing halt against a barrier of some kind. Backing up, she inspected it. Somehow its maker had hidden its magic. She twirled like a cyclone, narrowing her power to a fine point. Leaping at the barrier, she drilled her way through and continued on. She met another such barrier, and a third. They took even less time to penetrate than the first.

Once she was over the ship, she reached back to her body and called the sparks in her hair. She spun them as they left the land, shaping them into a single length. The bolt had almost reached her when a strange magical voice spoke in her mind.

Most impressive, lightning-girl. Still, I might look around, if I were you. Throw that bolt at me, and you will not like the consequences.

She had heard that cold, metallic voice before. Where?

Bit Island. Niko had been magicking her lenses, and a conversation had reached her ears. This speaker had told another, *Do your part, and your debt will be paid.*

The other's voice had been familar then, and no

wonder: it had been Aymery's. She ought to have known all along that her cousin was in trouble.

Don't blame him, child, advised the mage Enahar. *I fished very patiently for Aymery. I admit, I never expected him to bring me so important a catch as you.*

You murdered *him!* she cried.

As I will murder your friends if you do not keep your magic from me. Look again at my pattern.

She obeyed and saw to her horror that black threads had lashed Daja, Sandry, and Briar to the pattern of silver ones. Worse, Tris could see their magic bleeding off, coming her way. Coming to the pirate mage.

Don't worry, he said cheerfully. *Once they have rest, they'll be restored, and I can use them again. What a prize the four of you are! How strong, at such a young age! You shall have to explain how you managed to combine yourselves.*

I'll explain it to your bones, retorted Tris, trying to sound braver than she felt. She'd gotten her friends into this, rushing in—

But I didn't want them here! she thought desperately. I went by myself!

You knew—you guessed—they'd chase you, another part of her said. You knew the four of you could inflict *real* damage.

Your manners leave something to be desired. Those Life Circle milksops don't appear to realize that the young require discipline. Well, we have time to work on that. You owe me a considerable debt, my girl. The voice went even colder, if that was possible. *You killed my sister Pauha, when you turned lightning on her ship.*

Good, snapped Tris. *I'm glad.* Her friends looked like they were sleeping. She couldn't let any harm come to them!

Let my friends go and I'll serve you, she told him, thinking, I'll kill myself first.

Release such prizes? Don't be ridiculous!

Back on the wall, bony fingers pried open one of her hands, the one with Aymery's earring in it. They pressed something light into her palm and closed her hand again.

Niko had just given her the string. Her own lump—the one that reminded her of wet spring winds and thunder—lay directly in the earring's gold hoop. Tris placed her thumb squarely on top of it.

The presence of their teachers brushed her awareness. Lark wrapped Sandry's hand around a lump that felt like balls of yarn and shimmering silk. Frostpine did the same for Daja, steering her open-eyed body closer to Tris. Rosethorn helped Briar's body to connect with his own part of the thread circle.

Now, whispered Briar. The three captives thrashed against their bonds.

Again! cried Tris. Silver letters and veils of air rose from Enahar's ship. She didn't want them to touch her.

One, two, three! cried Daja. The captives threw themselves against their bonds. The magic that held them turned brittle and collapsed. They were free.

Enahar roared in fury. All around him the web of magic turned pale. He was drawing in power as he'd drawn it from Sandry, Briar, and Daja, bleeding his other mages to attack the four.

I don't think I have enough to fight with, Daja said nervously. *Frostpine? Help me?*

Broad hands gripped her shoulders. It felt as if the sun had just appeared behind her. *I thought you'd never ask,* he said.

Lark united with Sandry; Rosethorn with Briar. Tris waited, until she realized that Niko would not unite with her uninvited. *He has a cat's good manners,* she thought. To the sense of him in her mind she said, *Please?*

He attached his magic to hers. Once again the four became one, their strength increased a dozen times by the arrival of their teachers. Forming a blade of magic, all eight plunged down, hacking at the threads that connected Enahar to the mages of the cove fleet. Singly, then in clumps, the threads gave. Next Tris and her friends slashed his bonds to the mages before Summersea. Those ties parted, cutting Enahar off: He was on his own. He raised silvery shields, strong protections that would be hard to break.

Tris stretched out a hand. The lightning bolt had

stayed nearby while Enahar taunted her. Now it settled into her grip. To it Sandry fed the power of the spindle that had made the four into one. Briar added the green strength of stickers and thorns. From Daja came the white blaze of the harbor chain.

Tris pointed to Enahar's shields. *Strike*, she whispered.

The bolt split the air, giving birth to thunder. The shields, and Enahar's ship, exploded.

Shadow fingers locked around Tris, dragging her from Niko's hold.

If you want me so badly, you may go with me! the dying Enahar snarled. He clutched her tight, pulling the girl into darkness.

Lark and Sandry opened their real eyes on Winding Circle's wall. "There's something that binds her to him," said Lark. "A cord of some kind—"

Sandry pried open Tris's clenched fingers and lifted away the string circle to reveal a gold hoop. "Aymery's earring," she whispered.

Niko, looking gray, had returned to his own body. So, too, had Briar, Rosethorn, Frostpine, and Daja.

"I think I know what to do," said the Trader. She took the earring and placed it on the stone before her. A few sparks lingered still in Tris's hair; she collected those. Sandry gave them a spin, turning them into a small lightning bolt.

Briar gripped it and aimed it at the earring. "Strike," he, Daja, and Sandry whispered.

The bolt lashed the earring, turning it to a blob of liquid metal.

Tris yanked clear of Enahar as he faded to nothing. She rose from the pit he had dragged her into, until she found herself drifting on the sea's magical currents. Going back this way might take a while. She was too weak to move higher and steal a ride on breeze-back, but the tide would take her home.

Floating, she looked around and found horror. Overhead patches of battlefire burned on the surface, setting the remains of wrecked ships on fire. Other ships were in motion, trying to move out into the open sea, away from Winding Circle. Bodies floated everywhere, tangled in debris, some of them in flames.

The dead drifted in dozens to the sea's floor, weighted down by chains. Some of them were in pieces; some were burned. Some had been alive when they entered the water, and their faces were masks of panic.

The galley slaves, she realized. They had no way to free themselves. How many of them had she killed? And how many were guilty of nothing but being unable to escape—or fight back—when pirates came to call?

Power—Lark's—found her drifting among the dead. Encircling her like a net, it brought her home.

She heard cheering and opened her eyes. The other three children caught her as her knees wobbled, and she staggered. "What's the fuss about?" she asked through lips that felt swollen. Up here she could see the wreckage, survivors, and far too many bodies; they had begun to wash up on the beach. I can't take anymore, she thought, and closed her eyes.

"Look." Sandry eagerly pointed out to sea.

Raising her head, Tris looked.

It was the Emelan navy, coming down the peninsula. They had gathered as promised. The surviving pirates from the cove fleet were doing their best to escape before the duke's sailors had a chance at them.

"You'd better undo your waterspout," said Briar. "It'll make the duke mad if his ships are banged up."

With the navy's arrival, the deaths of their leaders, one fleet in pieces, and their wizards either directionless or in active revolt, the pirates waited for nightfall and fled. Some went directly into the navy's grasp; some got away. Duke Vedris promised his people that, as soon as was humanly possible, he would launch a force against the Battle Islands to burn the pirates out. Everyone knew they would come back, as they had for centuries, but law-abiding folk would have a few years of peace before they did.

For two days the children did nothing but eat and sleep, except for Tris, who also looked after her bird. Even if she had been able to slumber deeply, which she was not, his shrilling would have roused her.

Frostpine moved back to his room over his forge; Niko returned to his usual place.

On the third day, when she was up and around, Tris found Rosethorn minding her tomato plants. "I'm busy," the dedicate said crossly, tying a stem more firmly to its supporting stake.

Tris wasn't as frightened by this greeting as she would have been a week before. "I'd like to ask a favor, if I may."

Rosethorn tilted up her wide-brimmed hat in order to see Tris's face better. "The answer is no."

Tris half smiled. "Niko says he'll be in meetings here or in Summersea for a week. I want to help at the infirmaries in the afternoons, until my lessons start again. They need people to fetch water and food and so on. The only way I can do it is if someone looks after Shriek."

"Shriek?"

"That's what I'm calling him—because he does."

"I see." Rosethorn dusted a speck from a tomato. "Why the infirmaries?" she asked.

About to refuse to answer, Tris thought the better of it. "Lark said they took the pirate wounded. It's because of me some of them are here, so—I should help out."

"You'll hate it," commented Rosethorn. "There's smells—vomit, rotting flesh—a lot of them are burned. They won't thank you."

Lark had said the same. It wasn't that Tris didn't

believe them: she did. It just didn't change the fact that she had to do something to lay the ghosts of the floating dead who came in her dreams. "The first time in my life anybody thanked me for anything was after I came here. I'm not so used to it that I expect it from people."

Rosethorn adjusted a tie on a plant. "Just afternoons?"

Tris nodded.

"All right. Tonight you and I will talk about what happens to Shriek—Mila, what a name!—to Shriek next. He'll be ready to fly soon."

Tris nodded.

"Well, go on. Leave him in my workshop. I'll hear him just fine when he wants to be fed."

Rosethorn and Lark were right. It was not pretty in the infirmaries. The smell on the hot afternoons sent Tris out to be sick over and over. Burns had to be cleaned, the dirty bandages laundered in boiling water and hung out to dry. She carried buckets of water until her back, legs, and arms ached. The harsh soap they used reddened and cracked her hands. Every night Daja had to wake her when she fell asleep in her tub at the Earth Temple baths. No one thanked her except the healer-dedicates, and that only rarely. The pirate captives, who had the duke's justice to look forward to once they were better, snapped and taunted and yanked her curls or knocked things from her hands. The few slaves they had rescued only stared at the ceiling, wordless.

Three boom-stones had made it past the shields while Tris and her friends attacked the fleet. One had landed on a wing of the girls' main dormitory. The Water Temple dedicates finally barred Tris from working in that infirmary ward. She sparked lightning every time she set foot inside it.

On her eighth day of service, the dedicates sent their healed criminals to the duke's court in Summersea. Once they were gone, less than half of all the patients remained. With plenty of healers now to care for them, Tris was put to scrubbing the floor of a newly emptied room. She was half done when she heard a step. Looking up, she saw Niko.

"Are you ready to begin lessons again?" he asked.

She pushed her spectacles up on the bridge of her nose. "After I finish this floor."

"Have you any ideas about what area of your talents we should concentrate on?" It seemed like an idle question.

Her answer was not at all idle. "I need to learn control, Niko—for real. With everything. I think the rest has to wait." Swirling water fiercely in the bucket, she stared at soap bubbles to keep him from seeing her mouth tremble. She was beginning to fear she would dream about the drowned slaves for the rest of her life. "I don't want this to happen again. Not *ever*."

"At least you know it," he said quietly, rolling up

his sleeves. "You could have been another Enahar, living off human pain."

She looked up at him, her gray eyes sharp. "The other mages—were they *all* slaves? Aymery said as long as Enahar bound him with blood, he had to do what he was told. But . . . he liked the money, too, Niko. The money and the power. I could tell."

"Most of the mages served him willingly" was the quiet reply. "And had Aymery tried to disobey Enahar, he would have paid for it with even more of his blood."

"Dirty *jishen*," whispered the girl, scrubbing hard.

Niko tracked down a second brush and helped her finish the room.

Late that afternoon Tris was about to give Shriek a feeding at the big table when Briar carried a small, covered dish to her. Sandry and Daja followed—he'd hinted that a treat was in store.

"Rosethorn says to start giving him some of these," he informed Tris, offering her the container.

"Rosethorn?" Tris called.

"That's his natural food" was the reply from the workshop. "He won't survive when you set him free if you don't start him on this now."

Briar removed the lid on the dish with a flourish. Tris looked and shrank back. Inside squirmed one or two earthworms, a handful of grubs, and a small white caterpillar. Little Bear stood on his hind legs

248

to peer into the dish. Grabbing his collar, Daja hung on, in case the pup decided it was time to try bird food.

Shriek, still under the handkerchief on his nest, squalled.

"Drop them in his nest," Tris suggested to Briar.

"Can't. Rosethorn says they gotta go in his beak, same as the rest." Briar offered a small pair of metal tongs in the size that ladies used to pluck their eyebrows. "These'll help. Come on, bird-dam—he wants his supper."

"I *hate* bugs," insisted the girl. "They're—Shurri defend me, they *wiggle.*"

"Come on, merchant girl," said Daja with a grin. "You faced pirates, an earthquake, Rosethorn—what's wrong with a bug or two? Did she get any locusts?" the Trader asked Briar. "They're better fried, but still good when they're fresh."

Tris gagged.

"Nothing that flies is in there, or it'd be gone by now," Briar said. "Get to work, four-eyes. We haven't got till the end of time."

"Will you do it?" Tris begged Sandry. "You're not afraid of anything."

Sandry tucked her hands behind her back. "I'm not his mama," she replied with an evil grin.

"Neither am I!" cried Tris.

Briar put the tongs in her hand and wrapped her fingers around them.

"The caterpillar is crawling out," remarked Daja. She flicked it back into the dish.

"You do it!" Eagerly Tris thrust the tongs at her. "You like bugs!"

Daja grinned and stepped back. "Sandry's right. I'm not his mother, either."

None of them but Little Bear had paid attention to the nest-box as the handkerchief cover bumped, thrashed, and finally slid off. Its inhabitant climbed out. Almost a fledgling, Shriek was now three inches long from head to rump, with another two inches of tail. He was still in dull gray pinfeathers, but his black eyes were alert and wide open. He waddled across the table, yelling.

The dog fled. The four children watched Shriek.

"Maybe he'll eat from the dish," suggested Daja. She thrust it into his way.

Shriek walked around it without once shutting up, heading for Tris. When she stretched out her hand to him, he pecked one finger hard.

"Ow! Shriek—"

He screamed and pecked, again. Tris backed up.

Shriek came on and dropped off the edge of the table. Sandry and Tris banged into each other in their rush to catch him, while the bird—cradled in Sandry's skirt—continued to scream. When Tris gathered him up, he continued to peck her. She kept her hands cupped around him, wincing at the pain. "That beak is *sharp*," she complained.

"Anything for peace and quiet." Picking up the tongs, Briar selected a worm and held it over Shriek. The nestling gave Tris a last jab and sat up in her hands, opening his beak wide. Briar dropped the worm in. Shriek swallowed. He appeared to think about what he'd just eaten.

"Well, *that's* better, anyway," Sandry remarked with a sigh.

Shriek screamed.

"My turn." Daja took the tongs and offered the caterpillar to the bird. This Shriek bit in two, allowing her to keep half while he gulped down the rest. Once that tidbit was in his belly, he snatched the rest out of the tongs.

Sandry picked up an earthworm with her fingers. Shriek accepted this offering as he had the caterpillar, eating it in neat bites.

"Your turn, Mama." Briar drew the nest-box over so Tris could put her charge back in his bed. Shriek squalled.

Slowly, gingerly, Tris picked up a grub with the tongs, wincing as her firm hold crushed the sacrifice. She positioned the tongs over the nestling's gaping beak and dropped the grub in.

Everyone applauded. Shriek blinked, sighed, and settled down for a nap.

Tamora Pierce says she first got the idea for the Circle of Magic books by watching her mother and sister do needlework. "Seeing them knit, quilt, and crochet in the evenings, I often thought—as I eyed my two left hands—that what I witnessed was magic in our real world, the magic of turning thread and cloth into beautiful, useful things with little fuss or ceremony. That notion lodged in my brain. For years I fiddled with the concept of crafts magic, including a play, a short story, and mentions in a book that all dealt with thread magic.

"At the same time I was conducting those experiments, I became friends with an artist jeweler who, over the course of his long career, had turned his hand not only to weaving, sewing, and embroidery, but also to architecture, woodworking, pottery, glassblowing, and the smithing of all kinds of metals. Our friendship broadened my conception of magic expressed in crafts, while my initial fascination with magic worked in thread gave me a place to start. Offered the chance by Scholastic to create a new magical universe, I decided to get serious about crafts and their power, both real and imagined."

Tamora Pierce was born in western Pennsylvania, has lived in various states across the country, and currently resides in New York City with her husband. A graduate of the University of Pennsylvania, she has studied social work, film, and psychology. She has worked as head writer for a radio production company, martial arts movie reviewer, housemother in a group home, literary agent's assistant, and investment banking secretary. Today she is a full-time writer.

Ms. Pierce began to write at the age of eleven. Her first two fantasy cycles, The Song of the Lioness and The Immortals, are very popular with young readers and have won many honors. The Circle of Magic quartet—including *Sandry's Book*, *Tris's Book*, *Daja's Book*, and *Briar's Book*—has been hailed by reviewers as "gripping adventure" (*School Library Journal*) and "a rich and satisfying read" (*Kirkus Reviews*). Upcoming are four more books, called The Circle Opens, which will feature some characters familiar from the Circle of Magic as well as many new ones.

Inside the smithy, Daja could hear Polyam clearly. Eavesdropping, not thinking of what she was up to, Daja had gone to draw a fresh nail-rod out of the fire. Instead of one length of iron, she had grasped the entire fistful of rods she'd set to heat.

Once in her grip, unnoticed by Daja, the rods had twined around each other, then split apart, forming three branches. One branch reached toward the fire, splitting again to form three twigs. Another branch wound itself around Daja's arm.

Startled by the feel of iron on her skin—though she could handle red-hot metal without getting burned, the sensation was an odd one—Daja looked down. A third iron branch reached between the fingers on her free hand, then wrapped around her palm and over her wrist.

Daja tried to pull free and failed. She bent her power on the iron, silently ordering it back to its original shape. Instead the pieces that gripped her arms continued to grow. They each seized a shoulder, holding it fast. One spread down her back; another sprouted a tendril that gently twined around her neck. That was when she panicked and screamed.

When Tris reached her, she found Daja trapped by what looked like an ancient grapevine—trunk, limbs, and all—made of iron that still glowed orange with heat. It was sprouting metal leaves.

"It's *growing*," Polyam gasped. She had followed Tris back to the forge.

"I can see that!" growled Tris. "Now hush—I have to do some magic." *Frostpine!* she cried silently, calling through her magical connection to her friends. They needed Daja's teacher, and they needed him now.

"Briar, I need my glass," Rosethorn ordered. "And I want quiet, understood?"

"Yes, Lady," replied Alleypup.

Briar grinned—Rosethorn was always convincing—and took a velvet pouch from the workbag. Carefully he slid out its contents: a round lens four inches across, its edges bound in a metal band, fixed to a metal handle. He passed it to his teacher.

Rosethorn examined Flick, talking softly to her the entire time. At last the dedicate sat back, frowning. "When did you get sick, and how did this illness develop?"

Flick answered weakly. At last Rosethorn stood, holding the lens out for Briar to take. As he did, he saw that drops of sweat had formed like pearls on Rosethorn's pale skin. For all that she acted calm, she was upset, as upset as she'd ever been when facing pirates or forest fires.

For a moment she was silent. Finally she straightened her shoulders and back. "This will take arranging, I think. Briar, I need you to link me to Niko—I assume he's at the duke's with the girls. Getting Flick to Urda's House will be tricky."

When Flick opened her mouth to protest, Rosethorn glared at her, fisted hands on hips. "Something for you?" she asked ominously.

Flick shook her head and sank back on her rags. Briar grinned: He'd known Flick was smart.

"Has anyone else been here since you first got sick?" asked Rosethorn.

"Just me, and I been out and about," said Alleypup. "Nickin' food and the like."

"We'll need to make a list of everyone you saw, then," Rosethorn murmured, thinking aloud. "Briar? Have the girls link us with Niko, please."

Briar closed his eyes as Rosethorn wrapped her hands around his. Unlike talking to Rosethorn at Urda's house, speaking to any of the girls was easy. He only had to look for them in his own mind.

Circle of Magic #1: Sandry's Book

Circle of Magic #2: Tris's Book

Circle of Magic #3: Daja's Book

Circle of Magic #4: Briar's Book

The Circle Opens #1: Magic Steps

The Circle Opens #2: Street Magic

The Circle Opens #3: Cold Fire

The Circle Opens #4: Shatterglass

The Will of the Empress

Melting Stones

From #1 *New York Times* Bestselling Author

Tamora Pierce

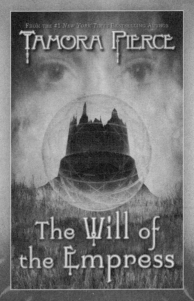

The epic reunion of the four mages from the Circle of Magic series.

Daja, Briar, and Tris join Sandry on a trip to visit her cousin, the Empress of Namorn. But the four mages haven't been together in some time and their magic isn't what it used to be. When the Empress's evil intentions are revealed, Sandry and her friends will have to learn to work together—before the Empress gets her way.

Scholastic Press